KINTALLOCH

Mercedes Clarasó

by the same author

fiction
Natana, a novel

translation
Weir de Hermiston i altres relats
(R. L. Stevenson's *Weir of Hermiston* in Catalan)

KINTALLOCH

A tale of Scottish family life

Mercedes Clarasó

BLACK ACE BOOKS

First published in 1994 by
Black Ace Books, Ellemford, Duns
Berwickshire, TD11 3SG, Scotland

© Mercedes Clarasó 1994

Typeset in Scotland by Black Ace Editorial

Printed in Great Britain by Antony Rowe Ltd
Bumper's Farm, Chippenham, SN14 6QA

A CIP catalogue record for this book
is available from the British Library

ISBN   1–872988–31–8

The publishers gratefully acknowledge
subsidy from the Scottish Arts Council
towards the production of this volume

For Ana María

1

The child came down the stairs slowly, solemnly.

This was the most important day in her life. For two years she had been looking forward impatiently to this birthday. She stopped on the landing half-way down the stairs and thought about the awesome fact. At last she was seven years old. And so, of course, was Tom. Only Tom didn't seem to feel the same way about it. He was excited, naturally; a year older, and then there would be the presents and the party.

All this mattered to him. Mattered more, Ellen felt, than it should, on this occasion. Parties and presents were, after all, trivial things. She had tried to bring home to him the importance of being seven. Not only were they now seven years old, but the year, 1877, had two more sevens in it. And this, surely, underlined the importance of being seven years old.

'Of course it's better to be seven than six,' he had conceded. 'But being eight will be even better still.'

'Oh, no!' she had cried, shocked. This was the ultimate blasphemy.

He looked at her, puzzled. 'But what's so special about being seven?'

She couldn't give a reason. 'It just is. Seven is the most special age you can ever be.' Then she added, 'Seven is the perfect number. I know because I heard Mama say so one day when they were reading tea cups.'

'Tea cups!' He turned away with scorn. 'Women's talk, that's what it is. I thought you'd know better.'

Ellen was deeply hurt. Not only was this solemn conviction of hers being challenged, but for the first time she became aware of a real difference of opinion between herself and her twin brother.

'It's the right age to be,' she insisted in an anguished voice.

'It *is* the perfect number. I don't want ever to stop being seven years old.'

Tom gave her a troubled look. Then he assumed his elder brother expression, put his arm round her shoulder and said:

'All right, Nellen, we'll be seven as long as we can. Agreed?'

She nodded.

That had been yesterday, the Day Before. Well, the rift had been healed, that was the main thing. But it was evident that Tom didn't feel the solemnity of the occasion as she did. Perhaps now that the great day had arrived the mere fact of being seven would bring its wisdom. She had no arguments she could put forward to convince him. Apart from her mother's statement about seven being the perfect number she could find no grounds for her certainty. But a heartfelt conviction needs no reasoning to support it, and up till yesterday she had never felt the need of any. It simply hadn't occurred to her that Tom might not feel the same as she did about so important a matter.

Now, standing half-way down the stairs, she prepared herself for the dignity that awaited her. Tom, as heir to the estate, had already been sent for by his father for their daily round of the stables and one of the estate farms. So Ellen would have to face the social start of the day, and of every day, without him. The real start of the day, of course, they had had together, while the others were still sleeping.

Would the rest of the family notice, would they realize, would they remember her new status? She took a deep breath and continued the journey down.

And it had been a wonderful birthday. She could sense that her parents were aware of how special the occasion was. Several times she felt obliged to nudge Tom and say, 'You see, I was right. It *is* different this year.'

And Tom had been unable to disagree. He too had felt a special something in his parents' behaviour. It wasn't like an ordinary day. Not even like an ordinary birthday, and he could remember several.

Once their father had talked about seven being a special age. 'Well on the way to being grown up,' he had said, and Tom and Ellen had exchanged looks of complicity. Yes, she felt sure that Tom was now convinced too. Her happiness was complete. This was a day she would remember all her life.

Just before bedtime there was a certain whispering and consultation between her parents:

'You!'

'No, you!'

The words recurred several times.

Finally Mama said, in a rather unsteady voice, 'Well, it's nearly time for bed, and there's one last surprise for you tonight. Now that you're both seven you're big enough to have a bedroom each. The servants have moved all your things into the two lovely new rooms which . . . '

She was interrupted by a loud, heartbroken wail from Ellen. 'But I want to sleep with Tom! I want to go on sleeping with Tom!'

At the same time Tom cried out, 'I don't want a room each! I want to stay in the nursery with Ellen!'

Discussing it later the twins realized that this must have been the reason for the suppressed excitement shown by their parents during the day. They were bound to know how their children would react to the new sleeping arrangements. Tom and Ellen had never been separated during the night, and hardly ever during the day, for that matter. Only lately had Andrew Lindsay started taking the boy about the estate without his little shadow. Both parents were becoming concerned about the apparent inseparability of the twins. For some time they had viewed with trepidation the prospect of separating them at night. But friends and other members of the family had hinted, and more than hinted, at the impropriety of letting the boy and girl sleep together any longer.

After the children, still screaming loudly, had been dragged to their rooms and firmly locked in, Andrew and Catherine faced each other, shaken but determined. It had to be done. They agreed that it might have been better to tackle the problem some years earlier. But every time they had thought about it in the past their courage had failed them. Having at last made a move, they felt they simply had to persevere. If they didn't, they realized from what people said, and from what they didn't say, that it could give rise to a pretty unpleasant situation. They couldn't allow the children to grow up with the stigma attached to . . . to that sort of thing. If people were talking already, what would it be like in another year or two? Sooner or later the children themselves would hear something. No, it had to be avoided, at all costs.

'Perhaps, though,' suggested Catherine, 'it was a mistake to choose their birthday.'

'Do you think so? What difference does it make?'

'Oh, just that it makes it all a bit more memorable. I wish we'd thought of that.'

'Well, anyway, we'll just have to see,' concluded Andrew.

Meanwhile, they heard. For a long time the screams reached them two floors down in the drawing room. At last silence reigned, and Catherine decided she would just tiptoe up and see if they were asleep. They were – curled up in each other's arms. Tom had managed to pick the lock of his room, and once outside Ellen's door all he had to do was turn the key in the lock.

Gradually the children came to accept their nocturnal separation, although they still managed to sleep together whenever anything had occurred to upset either. Their passionate attachment remained unshaken. But the spontaneity with which they expressed their affection, especially in front of other people, disappeared almost overnight. The one thing that had got through to them from the new situation was the conviction that there was something shameful in their relationship. They puzzled over this together, unable to see where they had gone wrong. They simply couldn't account for it, but the sense of shame was there. That, at any rate, had been achieved.

As they grew up, their affection remained as strong as ever. But the actual dependence on the other twin began to lessen as far as Tom was concerned. At home his father involved him more and more in the life of the estate, and when he was sent to boarding school his horizons widened yet again. Although he was by no means a scholar, he was a good all-rounder, popular with boys as well as with masters, and enjoyed life at school.

For Ellen it was pure loss. She had no new experience to fill the gap left by her brother when he was away at school, and no sense of a mission to fulfil at home. She grew timid and uncertain, lacking the support she had taken for granted in her early childhood.

One evening when the twins were twelve and Tom was home for Christmas, they were discussing the party from which they had just come. The others had teased Ellen about one of the boys there, who had shown a preference for her. At home Tom started teasing her again.

Ellen was affronted. 'No, I don't love Peter Jackson, and I won't marry him, and you know it. And it's cruel of you to tease me about him or about anyone. You know I can never marry, never, never.'

'Why not? What's to stop you?'

'Oh, Tom, how can you ask? You know very well why. It's because I can't marry *you*. Remember when we were little we used to say we'd marry each other? And now we know we can't. But I'll never, never marry anyone else.'

Tom was silent.

'What's the matter?' she asked. 'Would you like it if I married anyone else?'

'No, of course not. I'd hate it and I'd hate him. But I can't make the same promise, though I see you expect me to. But things aren't as simple as that.'

'What do you mean?'

11

'What I've just said. That I can't make the same promise.'

'Why not? If I can make it, why can't you?'

'Because, whether I like it or not, I'm going to have to marry *someone*.'

'Why? Whatever for?'

'Because Kintalloch needs an heir.'

'But it's got one. You're the heir, silly.'

'Yes, but afterwards? Who do I leave the estate to?'

Ellen was stunned. 'I never thought of that,' she replied in a small voice. For the first time she realised that the two great forces in her life, her love for Tom and her love for Kintalloch, were in conflict.

2

I must be walking too fast, thought Andrew. There's that breathlessness coming on again. He paused for a moment. Then he walked to the nearest five-bar gate and rested against it for a while. He wondered whether he should go on to the lodge gates. On the one hand there was the force of a lifelong habit – every morning, after visiting the stables and one of the farms, he always walked along the avenue to the lodge gates, then home again for breakfast. It was a habit he had started in childhood, as he went the rounds with his father, and he had continued it with Tom. On the other hand there was the fear that if he went on to the lodge gates he might not have the strength left to get him back up the long climb to the house.

And then what?

The lodge stood empty, there was no-one there to help him. He would be missed at breakfast, Catherine would be alarmed, she and Ellen would come in search of him, and he would have to tell them how ill he felt. No, he thought, I must try to keep going, I mustn't cause all that concern and alarm. It may, after all, just be a passing thing. Perhaps a touch of flu . . . The important thing is to keep going on as usual, at least till Tom finishes his degree. If I can hold out till then . . .

Slowly he started the return journey to the house. No-one need know that he had had to curtail his usual round.

As he approached the house Catherine saw him from her bedroom window. He was walking very slowly, far too slowly for him. Just then she heard the front door opening and saw Ellen running out to meet her father. As soon as he saw her he quickened his pace, evidently anxious to appear normal. By the time father and daughter had reached the house Catherine was downstairs, waiting for them. She saw that Andrew looked very pale. Ellen didn't seem to have noticed. Obviously Andrew didn't want anything said at that moment. Catherine decided she would ask him what was the matter after breakfast. But he managed to slip out while she was talking to one of the servants. She didn't see him slip back into the house by the library french windows. Perhaps he wasn't feeling too bad after all, she thought, if he'd gone out into the grounds again.

But half an hour later one of the maids came to say that her master was sitting in the library. This in itself at that time of the morning was unusual enough. But the funny thing was, he was just sitting there, staring straight ahead of him, as if he didn't see her. It had given her quite a turn, she said, and thought she'd better report the matter.

Catherine ran down to the library, in a state of terrible apprehension. She was afraid she might find him dead. The relief of seeing him still alive was marred by the fact that he looked so ill. Without waiting for an argument she sent for the doctor at once. Dr Murdo was an old family friend, in whom they had the greatest confidence. After examining the patient he stood for some time with his back to the fire, stroking his beard thoughtfully, as if perplexed about what to say. Catherine looked from him to her husband's recumbent figure on the couch, then back again to the doctor. She became intensely aware of a feeling that time was standing still. In later years, whenever she thought of this moment, this same impression of arrest came back. She was never able to decide how long the silence had lasted – a minute, five, ten?

By the following day they had decided that Tom must be sent for. Anxious as his parents were not to interrupt his studies, they both had a strong sense of continuity with regard to the estate. If Andrew was no longer able to look after it (and the doctor's diagnosis left no hope of that), then someone else must take charge of things as soon as possible, and Tom should be given the chance to do it. If he decided to stay on at college and finish his course (and a degree in law might be a useful addition to the skills required to run the estate), then someone else must be engaged.

14

They spent a long time trying to find the right formula for the telegram, something that could have the desired effect of bringing Tom back right away, without alarming him unduly. In the end they settled for:

NEW SITUATION ARISEN STOP PLEASE COME FOR CONSULTATION.

Ellen, of course, who knew about the doctor's visit, had been told already how seriously ill her father was, and now awaited Tom's arrival with a mixture of sorrow, fear and elation. If Tom were to decide to come home for good, and she was sure this would be his reaction, then her fondest dream would have come true. The disappointment of his not getting his degree would be a small price to pay for the knowledge that he would now make his home for ever where he belonged, in Kintalloch, beside her. But how sad that her father's health, perhaps even his life, should be the price of Tom's return.

Ellen had never forgotten her seventh birthday, the misery of separation from Tom, the shock of learning that somehow or other their love was tinged with shame. Now, at twenty-one, she had learned enough to appreciate the dilemma her parents had been in. While the spontaneous trust of childhood had been shattered, she had managed to retain a certain dogged and dutiful love for both of them, and she grieved for them in their distress.

As soon as he got the telegram Tom realized he must go home right away. He spent most of the journey trying to decide what could be the matter, and felt pretty certain that the 'new situation' must have something to do with his father's health. During the previous vacation he had noticed that his father was walking more slowly, and often seemed breathless. Long before reaching home he had decided what action to take, if this was the problem. On hearing the facts he refused to listen to his father's suggestion that he go back and finish the term before coming to any decision. He insisted that he had already made up his mind, that Kintalloch came before anything else, and that he was staying there, from that very moment onwards. He would write to his professor explaining the situation, he would get a friend to pack his things, and a servant should be sent to collect them. Thus in a few moments did he dispose of his whole university career. Neither of his parents was able to alter his decision.

Not that Catherine tried very hard.

She had a feeling that Andrew had little time left, and the presence of this eager and capable son would, she knew, be a great comfort to them all. Although she realized that Tom was as devoted to his sister as ever, she had never sensed the suspicion and hostility in him that Ellen had often evinced since that disastrous birthday. And so she felt more at ease with Tom, more able to relax and let him take over the running of the estate.

When the discussion was over, and Tom's decision accepted, they agreed that the first person to be told should be Ellen. She was sent for, and came in looking anxious and tense. Both her parents saw the wild flame of joy in her eyes when she heard of Tom's decision, and both felt a certain sense of foreboding. As soon as the young couple had left the room Andrew turned to his wife. 'Did you see?'

She nodded. 'You'd better tell him soon,' she said.

'Yes,' he agreed, 'it's the nearest we can get to a guarantee.'

Neither parent had ever found out what exactly was the relationship between the twins. Perhaps they never really wanted to know. In all their discussions it was understood that the real danger was public opinion. There was no doubt that tongues had wagged on occasion. Not only were they grieved by the possible misery this might bring to their two children, but they were affronted at the thought that any breath of criticism should sully the fair name of the Lindsays of Kintalloch. The best remedy they could think of was marriage, certainly for Tom (after all, there was also the question of the heir), but preferably for Ellen too. She might not make a happy marriage, but both parents were convinced that no woman is happy as an old maid, and wanted to avoid this fate for their daughter.

The urgent thing, however, was Tom's marriage.

The following day father and son had a lengthy discussion, in the course of which Tom agreed that he must marry, and marry soon. On the whole he had no strong objections, since it was clear that he was to make his own choice. But he was most apprehensive of the effect that this decision would have on Ellen. She had continued to maintain that she would never marry. As to his marrying, she agreed in principle that it would be required of him for the good of Kintalloch. But how would she take the thought of his marrying in the near future, especially now that she had allowed all her hopes to blossom with Tom's return to the fold? He knew she was looking forward to a resumption of the close relationship they had enjoyed before, when they did everything together and were always in each other's company. He felt that courtship *à trois* would be rather an impracticable proposition.

His fears about Ellen's reaction turned out to be fully justified. Ellen was shocked, hurt, indignant, tearful, and passionately opposed to the idea. In the end she had to yield to the facts, but only after he had promised that he would never marry any woman without Ellen's previous approval. For some time after obtaining this promise Ellen felt she had won the battle. All she had to do was to keep on rejecting any proposed candidate. But as her father's health deteriorated her attitude softened. She realised what a great relief it would be for both parents if Tom were married, and decided that she would seriously try to accept the girl of his choice.

The choice, as it turned out, was not so much his as that of his bride.

3

For the past week the main subject of conversation among the young ladies of Kintalloch village had been the forthcoming ball. The group gathered in Dr Murdo's sitting room was no exception. The two daughters of the house, Chrissie and Bessie, were entertaining friends, and all aspects of the ball were under discussion, not least the possible choice of partners. Tom Lindsay had danced with Chrissie several times at the last ball, and the general opinion was that she would again be so distinguished.

She tossed her head. 'Well, I don't care if he does – or if he doesn't. I've plenty of other partners to choose from.'

'Not quite so eligible as that, surely!'

'And what's so specially eligible about Tom Lindsay, I'd like to know?'

'Oh, hoity-toity!' exclaimed her sister. 'So the Lindsays of Kintalloch aren't good enough for the likes of us? That's news, surely.'

'The family's well enough.'

'Well enough! They're the best family in the district, everybody knows that,' exclaimed one of the guests.

'Yes, I know, I'm not arguing about that. It's just those two. I don't want to be mixed up in that sort of thing.'

One of the girls had only just come to the district and knew nothing about the local gossip. 'What sort of thing?' she enquired eagerly.

After much raising of eyebrows she was given to understand that there was something odd about the relationship between the twins.

The newcomer gasped with delighted horror.

'Oh, you don't mean . . . ?'

Bessie broke in:

'Yes, she does. And I don't believe a word of it. I don't know why people have to be so ill-natured. And if he asks *me* to dance I'll certainly accept.'

'And if he asks you to marry him, will you accept that too?' There was just a touch of spite in her elder sister's voice.

'I think I just might.' Bessie looked thoughtfully at the fire for a moment. Then she lifted up her dark, curly head and looked her sister in the eye. 'Actually,' she said, 'I wouldn't at all mind being mistress of Kintalloch. I think,' she went on, her brown eyes sparkling with mischief, 'I think I'll set my cap at him.'

'Pay no attention to her,' said Chrissie to the others, 'she's daft. I simply can't get her to take anything seriously. She's not showing any signs at all of growing up.'

Bessie stood up suddenly and started dancing round the room. 'I'm owre young tae marry yet, I'm owre young tae marry yet,' she sang. Then she stopped suddenly and said:

'But I'm going to have a jolly good try.'

'Who's that walking down the drive, Nellen?'

'It's Bessie. Bessie Murdo,' she added in explanation.

'Oh, her! Chrissie's sister, you mean? What's she doing here?'

'She came to see me.'

'Since when have you been friendly with her?'

'Since last week. She was very nice to me at the ball. Which is more than I can say of her sister,' she added with a touch of asperity.

Tom's evident admiration of the elder sister filled her with misgiving. If he should decide that this was the girl he wanted to marry, then they must have a battle. On no account could she possibly give her consent.

Tom decided to ignore the reference to Chrissie.

'So Bessie's taken a liking to you, has she? I wonder why.'

'Can't you guess?'

'Just your irresistible charm, I suppose,' he teased.

'No, yours.'

Tom raised his eyebrows, then laughed and shook his head. 'Don't be silly, Nellen.'

'I'm not. And she isn't either. She's taken a fancy to you, and knows she won't get anywhere if I disapprove. Well,' she conceded, 'perhaps that's putting it a bit strongly. But she's a bright girl, and she realizes that a friendship with me would be quite a convenient stepping-stone.'

'And you don't mind?'

'I'd much rather have her as a sister-in-law than Chrissie, if that's what you mean.'

'Actually, it wasn't. What I meant was, don't you mind being used in this way?'

'Not really. I'd rather be a stepping-stone than an object of contempt.'

'And that, you think, is how Chrissie regards you?'

'I know it is.'

'Because Bessie told you?'

'Bessie has never mentioned the subject. She knows she doesn't need to. I happen to have first-hand information as to how Chrissie feels about me, and Bessie was a witness. It was at the ball, when I went up to the cloakroom to take my things off. There was a crowd of girls there, and I could hear Chrissie's voice as I went up the stairs. She was speaking very loudly, in that scornful voice of hers. I couldn't make out what she was saying till, just as I entered the room, I heard the words, " . . . that precious twin sister of his." And the tone was even more scathing than the words. And just then she saw me, and they all did, and they were all terribly taken aback. Chrissie went bright scarlet and turned away, and all the others were struck dumb with embarrassment. It was Bessie who recovered her composure first, and came over and welcomed me in the most natural manner. She's very young and full of fun and high spirits, but I think she's got quite a lot of *savoir vivre*.'

'Enough at least to realize the value of cultivating your

friendship if, as you suggest, she's taken a fancy to me – or to Kintalloch, which is more likely.'

'Don't be so modest.'

'Well then, let's leave it that the two of us, Kintalloch and I, are more than any girl's heart can withstand. And if you have set your seal of approval on the match it but remains for me to fall in love with the girl and all will be well.' He spoke banteringly.

She answered in the same tone:

'You don't need to go to extremes. Simply marrying her will do.'

In spite of the lightness of their tone, they both knew that some of the most serious business of their lives had been settled in that conversation.

Three months later Bessie and Tom were married. By the time they came back from the honeymoon Andrew was so seriously ill that Catherine gave up all her normal duties in the house. Ellen and Bessie took over. But it was soon evident that Bessie had all the domestic and organisational skills that Ellen so obviously lacked. By the time Andrew died, a few weeks later, Bessie had taken over completely and Ellen had retired dreamily into the shadows, relieved at being able to drop the domestic burden, while at the same time mortified by her own ineptitude.

Soon after the funeral Catherine announced that she meant to take up residence in the disused lodge. She had no heart to resume her normal duties in the big house now that Andrew was gone, and she felt it was better for the young people to have the house to themselves, without the added cloud of her sorrowing presence. It was enough that they should have to start their married life with a bereavement. To have to put up with a recently widowed mother as well seemed an unnecessary hardship. The joy of youth, she felt, would reassert itself sooner without her. It was right that they should look forward; all she wanted to do was to relive the past.

Ellen's future now had to be decided. Her mother assumed that she would come with her to the lodge. Tom and Bessie thought that she should stay with them. Ellen herself simply didn't know what she wanted. Neither solution seemed satisfactory to her. She had never felt close enough to her mother to relish living with her in the tiny lodge. On the other hand, living with Tom and Bessie was also rather a strain. She tried hard not to be jealous; but it was clear that the young couple got on very well together, and she sensed their happiness and felt it as an affront. She was even hurt by the fact that Bessie seemed as keen as Tom – for her to stay with them. It seemed to underline the unity of the couple and the security Bessie felt in her position. In spite of her liking for Bessie, Ellen would have liked to see her less confident, less assured of the harmony between herself and her husband. In short, Ellen couldn't help feeling, and hating herself for the thought, that Bessie's happiness detracted from hers.

When she heard, in the usual circuitous way, that rumours about her and Tom were still circulating, she made up her mind.

'I'd better go, Tom,' she said. 'If I go and live in the lodge with Mama at least they'll have to stop talking.'

'I disagree. They'll just take it as a victory. The best proof that there's nothing wrong would be to have you living here happily with Bessie and me.'

Ellen winced at the word 'happily'. She felt that was an overstatement, at least as far as she was concerned. 'Is that why you want me to stay?' she asked bitterly.

'Oh, Ellen, Ellen, how could you think that?'

'You never call me "Nellen" now. Why? Orders?'

He sighed and shook his head. 'You know she's not like that. And I thought you liked her, anyway.'

'I do. But that doesn't alter the fact that she's taken you away from me. I know, I know,' she exclaimed, brushing aside his protests. 'With the best will in the world, and with my full consent. But it hurts all the same. Especially in little things like that. Why am I not "Nellen" any more?'

'That was a childish thing. We're grown up now.'

'Yes. As a married man you have put away childish things. You've had to, I suppose.'

'We all have to.'

Ellen went to live with her mother at the lodge. It had been added to and renovated, and made quite a comfortable dwelling for the two women. But she found the place claustrophobic, not so much because of its size as because of her mother's withdrawn state of mind, and she spent a lot of her time at the big house.

And it was there that she met Donald Crombie.

4

Donald had been a fellow student of Tom's.

The two men wanted to keep up the friendship and, as Tom found it difficult to get away from Kintalloch for visits to Edinburgh, Donald started coming for the weekend now and then. From the first he was attracted to Ellen. Apart from her cool, Nordic type of beauty, he admired her for the very qualities that she regretted in herself – her quiet, remote manner, her coolness, her timidity. Many people thought her proud, or insipid, or both. Donald had a suspicion that beneath the apparent indifference lay a passionate nature, and he dreamed of awakening this sleeping beauty. If only she could be made to feel love, he thought, how she would respond – little knowing that the awakening had taken place once and for all, many years ago.

Ellen liked Donald, and was flattered by his evident admiration. So far she had not received a great deal of male attention, partly, no doubt, because of the rumours that circulated about her and her brother, partly because this situation had undermined her self-confidence, and the only way she had learned to cope with society was by adopting this distant, indifferent manner. So it was very pleasant to be so obviously admired by this very presentable young man, with his dark good looks and his enthusiasm and vitality. But that was as far as it went. She still stuck to her initial determination never to marry, and made it so clear to Donald that she valued him as a friend, and as a friend only, that he was afraid of saying anything that might occasion a rebuff.

For Donald had his pride too, although it never came to the surface, and he was not considered proud. But he knew himself well enough to realize that a refusal from Ellen would be the end of their relationship. Besides, he told himself, he wasn't really in a position to marry yet. He had finished his studies and was now beginning to establish himself in the legal profession. So he worked hard, spent weekends at Kintalloch, and dreamed of the day when he would be able to offer Ellen a position so brilliant that she might be tempted to accept him.

In the end it was not Donald's position so much as the situation at Kintalloch that prompted Ellen to think seriously of marrying him. After several years of a happy but childless marriage, Bessie confided her news to Ellen one evening. 'I wanted to tell you myself,' she said. 'No-one else knows so far. I'm sure your mama will be pleased.'

'Yes, of course,' murmured Ellen, wondering why Bessie had wanted to tell her in person. Why not Tom? Presumably he knew, and surely they both realized that she would have preferred to be told by him? Besides, it was a family matter – an heir for the Lindsays of Kintalloch! Looked at from that point of view, it really had very little to do with Bessie, she told herself. Bessie was only the instrument. This was a Kintalloch affair.

After she had gone home and told her mother the news she sat for a long time by the fire, trying to analyse the feeling of something almost like anger in her heart. In the end she was able to name the emotion that was disturbing her.

It was jealousy.

The thought that another woman was going to bear Tom's child hurt her deeply. So that was the problem. In addition she had to admit that the presence of the child would draw husband and wife closer together, while it would push the unmarried sister further and further into the background. Better perhaps, she thought, to give up the role of unmarried sister, and let Donald see that his patience might be rewarded.

She hesitated as the weeks and months went by, unable to make up her mind to leave Kintalloch. It was Bessie who precipitated the decision. Bessie, whose delight in her pregnancy was so patent and so liberally shared with all and sundry, that the somewhat prudish Ellen was discountenanced on more than one occasion. She foresaw an endless succession of personal details, both before and after the birth, and decided that she could not go on living at Kintalloch. It'll have to be Donald, she told herself.

She felt no qualms about leaving her mother, recognizing that the two women had little to offer each other. Catherine lived almost entirely in the past, her daughter more or less in limbo – neither in the present nor the future, and yet feeling that she had been exiled from her past. Her mother, she was sure, would not miss her. Besides, she knew that both her parents had always hoped she would marry. As for Tom . . . He was still deeply attached to her, of that she felt sure; but he had his commitment to his wife, and now there would be the child . . .

Tom, she decided regretfully, would probably be relieved if she were to marry. And then she remembered her promise. It was she herself who had insisted that she would never marry. She reminded herself that the only person who knew of the promise was Tom, and that he probably wouldn't hold her to it. That didn't absolve her, of course. But still . . .

It would just be her own conscience she had to come to terms with. The action would harm no-one. In fact, it would bring happiness to Donald, satisfaction to her mother, and simplify the situation at Kintalloch. In a way, it seemed, it was her duty to break her promise. She wondered whether she was being Jesuitical or just realistic. It was a promise she should never have made in the first place. And if that was the case, where then did her duty lie?

She decided she would leave it to Tom. If he cared so little that he was prepared to see her become the wife of another man, then she had better go. But what if he objected? What if he reminded her of her promise and reproached her for her unfaithfulness? At the thought of this possibility her heart gave a great leap, and she realized that this was what she really wanted – to stay here with Tom because he really wanted her to stay, because he couldn't bear the thought of her belonging to another man. If that were really so, then she would put up with everything else – her own insignificant position, the prospect of being pushed even further into the background by the new arrival, even Bessie's exuberant motherhood, all these would be as nothing if she had the assurance that Tom still cared enough to try to keep her from belonging to another man.

When she told him of her idea Tom sat very still for a while. Then he asked, 'Is this really what you want?'

'No, it's not what I want. But it may be the best I can hope for.'

Another pause. 'Well, I suppose that's what you had better do. We'll miss you,' he added.

Ellen was deeply hurt. So that's that, she thought. I don't suppose he meant it, but that 'we' was as good as a slap in the face. 'We' always used to be *us*, Tom and me. And now, without even noticing, he uses it for his wife and himself. Even if he'd tried, he couldn't have shut me out more completely.

She realized now how much she had been hoping that her suggestion would bring her closer to Tom. She knew, of course, that they could never go back to the closeness of before. But she had hoped for some indication that Tom too longed for the union that had been theirs in the past. Now she knew that Tom was living in the present and in the future. The past hardly existed for him any more.

So, she would break her promise. She would marry Donald. But she promised herself that in her heart of hearts she would remain faithful to the faithless Tom. Whatever happened, she would never allow herself to love her husband. This second promise, she hoped, would relieve her of some of the burden of breaking the first.

Next morning she got up dry-eyed and resolute, if somewhat uncertain as to how to put her plans into execution. Having systematically held Donald at arm's length for so long, she didn't quite know how to let him understand that the ban had been lifted. How, she wondered, does a well brought up young woman let a man know that his advances will be welcome? No doubt the language of flirtation had its ways, but it was a language she had never learned and had no intention of learning.

Donald came that weekend, and she still hadn't thought of a way of approaching the subject. She would just have to trust to the inspiration of the moment. She made a start by asking him to go for a walk with her. They had often had walks together, but this was the first time the suggestion had come from her.

Donald was a lively conversationalist, a fact for which she had always been thankful. She found conversation difficult, and was always glad to play the part of listener, even though she listened with little attention, too engrossed in her own inner dialogue most of the time. Today, however, she could have wished for a little silence from Donald to let her get the conversation going in the right direction. At last she broke in while he was giving a lively account of that week's events in the law courts.

'I'm glad you came this weekend,' she said. 'I wanted to see you before going away.'

'Going away?' he repeated, as surprised by the information as by her abrupt manner of imparting it. 'Where are you going?'

'I don't know.'

For once Donald was speechless. Had something terrible happened? The thought of her leaving Kintalloch seemed inconceivable. That, in fact, had been one of the difficulties. He thought of her as so wedded to Kintalloch that the prospect of having to live in Edinburgh, were she to marry him, must seem unacceptable to her. And now she was planning to leave, without even a destination in mind! He could think of no possible reason for her decision, but it occurred to him that this might be his opportunity. He hesitated. Was this the moment for a proposal?

They walked on in silence, while Donald tried to decide whether to speak of marriage at this point, or to enquire further. He was not given to hesitation, but this matter was so important to him that he was afraid of spoiling everything by speaking too soon.

It was Ellen, however, who broke the silence:

'I know it must seem an odd decision to you. The fact is, I don't quite know how it's come about, but I've suddenly felt the conviction that I can't stay here any longer. I'm not needed at the lodge – Mama is living a life of her own, almost entirely in the past. I'm not needed at Kintalloch. And I'll be even less needed once the child arrives. I feel I ought to make some sort of life for myself. Only, I don't know what, or where.'

At this point she stopped and held out her hands in a gesture of helplessness. Donald stood in front of her and thought of all the fine speeches he had rehearsed. He'd even toyed with the idea of getting down on his knees, in the conventional manner. Looking at the November mud on the path he decided that part of the proceedings was out. As for the speeches, all he could manage in his surprise was:

'You could marry me, you know.' As a proposal he had to admit it lacked elegance. It seemed almost casual.

And her reply, 'Yes, I suppose I could,' seemed equally casual. She turned abruptly and started walking again. After a moment's hesitation, while he tried to decide how to take her answer, he caught up with her.

Had she accepted him? he wondered.

It was a point that had to be settled before they got back to the house. But it seemed ridiculous to have to ask her. Perhaps this was the occasion for one of the fine flights of amatory rhetoric that he had so often rehearsed – suitably amended, of course. The 'This may come as a great surprise to you' bit would have to go, naturally. Salvation, it seemed, lay in this course. It would ensure that some parts of the fine speeches he had thought up could be delivered, it would clarify the situation – at least he would then know whether they were engaged – and it would break the prolonged silence, which she must find odd, if indeed she considered that she had just pledged herself to him in marriage.

He was still choosing his opening words when Ellen broke the silence again:

'When do you think we should get married?'

Just before going into the house Donald stopped and asked:

'Am I permitted to mention our engagement?'

'Oh, yes.' Her voice sounded almost indifferent.

'In that case I'll see Tom right away.'

'Oh, no – not Tom!' All the indifference had vanished from her voice, and she put a hand on his arm as if to stop him.

'But I thought, as head of the family, Tom . . . '

'No, no,' she increased the pressure on his arm in her urgency. 'It's Mama you ought to see first . . . I'll tell Tom myself. But you must speak to Mama.'

He wasn't sure that she'd got the family priorities right, but he respected her for what he took to be her scrupulous insistence on her mother's rights in the matter. 'Of course,' he said, 'I'll see your mother first.' And gently, lightly, he laid his fingers on her hand as it still rested on his arm.

So nothing was said at the time to Tom and Bessie.

When Ellen left and Donald accompanied her as usual down the long dark avenue to the lodge, Tom sat thoughtfully gazing at the fire. He felt sure the matter had been settled, but could say nothing about it to Bessie without reference to his previous conversation with Ellen. The whole subject of his relationship with his sister was one he could never discuss with his wife, out of loyalty to Ellen. Bessie herself had never mentioned the matter. And yet he knew, from Ellen, that she had heard the rumours. This silence was a source of pain and discomfort to both of them. Bessie would have liked him to speak, to assure her that there was no truth in the rumours. But then, perhaps he would not be able to give her this assurance. Perhaps that was why he kept silent. Or it might simply be that he hoped she had heard nothing and didn't want to upset her with so scurrilous a breath of scandal.

Bessie suddenly broke the silence. 'I think there's something going on between those two,' she said. 'Didn't you notice anything?'

'What sort of anything?' he hedged.

'Just a sort of tension. Do you think Ellen might have relented at last?' Then she laughed. 'I hope he can afford an efficient housekeeper. Can you see Ellen running a house?'

Shortly before the wedding Ellen realized that this aspect of her new life was going to be no laughing matter. It suddenly came to her that she would be in charge of this strange house, with a staff of completely unknown servants, in a city she hardly knew and cordially disliked – disliked merely on the strength of its being a city.

Apart from the brief spell during the last days of her father's illness, she had never had to give any thought to what goes on in a house. Even now, in the lodge, her mother took charge of everything, helping their one servant when necessary, making all the decisions, ordering all the supplies. How was she to cope with all this, on so much larger a scale? How could she be sure to run things according to Donald's standards, when she didn't even know what these standards were?

She suddenly realized she had never seen Donald in his own surroundings. By the eve of the wedding she was in such a panic that she told Donald they'd better call it off. Donald laughed with relief when he heard the cause of the trouble. In the end he managed to calm her by promising that he would help her in every possible way.

'And you'll make all the decisions, won't you?' she insisted.

'If you like. But people will think I'm a terrible tyrant, you know. Still, if it makes you happier, then just tell everyone that you'll consult me before deciding, even if it's only a matter of the colour of the bathroom curtains.'

With that reassurance Ellen decided she could just about face married life. All decisions were referred to Donald. At first this was of vital importance, for she had no knowledge about anything in her province. Gradually, as her understanding of the business of housekeeping and entertaining grew, she found this consultation no longer necessary, but clung to it all the same. It was a way of preserving her indifference to all that surrounded her.

5

Ellen's marriage was something she endured, but got little satisfaction out of. Both by nature and by profession, Donald led a very sociable life, with a wide circle of acquaintants, and they did a lot of entertaining during the early years of their marriage. Ellen hated having to meet strangers, and never seemed to get beyond the stage of pleasant civilities, so the social life was a constant trial to her. But she understood how necessary this aspect of things was for Donald, and did her best, always uncertain beneath her appearance of calm formality, always longing for the moment when she could be alone again and give herself up fully to her own thoughts.

And yet her thoughts were seldom pleasant, and never encouraging. The first few years of her marriage went by in a sort of dreary dream. And then came her pregnancy, and the hope that things would change. Her daughter was born shortly before her thirtieth birthday, on the first of January 1900. A new century and a new life, she thought. Perhaps I shall recover my other half now.

Donald felt he had no reason to complain of the marriage. He had never expected Ellen to return his love. It was enough that she accepted it. He had got what he had bargained for – a wife who was beautiful, distinguished and, if not universally liked, at least admired and respected. He had an active and inquisitive turn of mind, and was amused and entertained by the variety of small domestic and social matters that were continually being brought to him for arbitration. He had heard nothing of the rumours concerning Ellen and Tom, and had never understood why his wife should be so diffident. After all, she came from a higher social class than he did, and could have been expected to feel completely at ease in most situations. It seemed odd that she should be continually consulting him about all sorts of domestic and social matters – what to wear on any given occasion, which invitations to accept and which to give, etc. He put it down to her consciousness of the fact that she had been brought up exclusively in the country, allied to her natural reticence and unwillingness to be in the limelight. He soon saw that her habit of turning every situation into a ritual was a form of opting out of any successive decisions to be made, and accepted this way of life for her sake, although personally he would have preferred a more spontaneous approach.

Donald had the quick wits and the self-confidence to be able to cope with most situations, and enjoyed the challenge of the unexpected. At the same time, he had known Ellen long enough before they were married to foresee what things would be like. He was sufficiently fair-minded to understand that his lack of foresight was his fault, not hers. Having succeeded in marrying the woman of his choice, he would have been unreasonable to expect her to behave out of character. At first he had hoped that time would convert her into the poised, calm hostess that her position, or rather his, demanded. In the end he had to admit that she had managed to produce a very good imitation. It was only the few people behind the scenes who had any idea of the effort that this calm appearance cost her. He often wondered at the tenacity with which she stuck to her role, at her uncomplaining acceptance of the social round imposed on her. He assumed it was part of her innate sense of duty, and admired her for it. And he was right – only this sense of duty was coming into play as the result of a series of promises of which he knew nothing – first her promise never to marry, then the promise she substituted in its place, never to love her husband, and thirdly, the promise that her sense of guilt towards Donald had forced upon her, that she would do everything in her power to be a good wife.

Ellen had never thought of herself as the maternal type, but she found to her surprise that she quickly became absorbed in the baby. Donald, in his turn, had never felt that founding a family was high on his list of priorities – he was too concerned with his career and the social life that this engendered. But the presence of this tiny creature that was a part of himself filled him with awe, and he spent many hours simply looking at the baby and listening to what Ellen had to say about how it had spent the day. This was the one subject on which she became communicative, and it brought husband and wife closer together. For the first time they had a love in common. Donald spent more time quietly at home with his wife and daughter, and, to Ellen's relief, they entertained rather less.

His colleagues and acquaintances would smile indulgently whenever he spoke of the child. It was clear that he thought he had quite the most beautiful and gifted child ever to appear on the face of this earth. Used to be quite a ladies' man, they would say, remembering his past reputation. And just look at him now. The perfect family man.

In his bachelor days Donald had indeed acquired a reputation as a lover of the ladies. Even after meeting Ellen and falling in love with her, he still pursued his amours with undiminished ardour. Ellen had made it so plain that she would have none of him, that he felt he was entitled to consolation where he could get it. As long as she remained the *princesse lointaine* this state of affairs continued. But from the moment that she agreed to become his wife he decided that this was to be the end of his philandering, and he stuck to his decision.

One evening when little Meg was about five years old Ellen heard her husband coming in and went to meet him in the hall. As he took off his coat he asked, 'Are the Hillyards coming this evening?'

'Oh, yes. I thought I'd told you. Everyone accepted. We'll have a full table.'

This was a situation that normally gave Donald great satisfaction. Having fought his way up from the ranks, as it were, it was a constant source of joy to him to sit at the head of a well appointed table, with a collection of well dressed, successful guests on either side of him, and a beautiful and distinguished-looking wife at the far end. Today, however, all he did was emit something between a grunt and a sigh.

'Why, what's the matter?'

'Oh, nothing. It's just that Walter Hillyard and I had a bit of a brush in court this morning. I had hoped he would have had the grace to make some sort of excuse and stay away.'

'Well, I'm afraid he hasn't. If they weren't coming they'd have sent word by now. What happened, anyway?'

'He accused me of having forgotten to send him an important document. He really got quite heated about it. And then it turned out that I hadn't forgotten it and that he had it among his papers after all. And he had to apologize, of course. It wouldn't have mattered if the whole thing hadn't been so public. I've a feeling he's out for my blood.'

'But why, if the whole thing was his fault?'

Donald made a wry face. 'Well, perhaps I wasn't as gracious about it as I might have been.'

Knowing her husband's gift for acerbity, Ellen nodded. 'I see,' she said, hoping they weren't going to have too difficult an evening. For once she felt glad that it was to be a large gathering. 'They say there's safety in numbers,' she offered in consolation. 'Surely he won't want to make an exhibition of himself in front of all the others.'

'No, I suppose not. Let's hope you're right.'

In fact the evening started off very well. Walter Hillyard looked slightly less at his ease than usual, but that was all. As the dinner progressed Ellen noted with satisfaction that Donald was beginning to look more relaxed. She was glad he had told her about the little problem. Since Meg's birth she had felt that they were gradually coming closer to each other. Not that she was in any danger of breaking her second promise and falling in love with him. Nothing like that. But a little more communication between them made it easier for her to carry out her third promise. The fact that he had told her about the unpleasant scene in court seemed to show that perhaps she really had succeeded in becoming a good wife to Donald. In spite of a slight nervousness about any disagreeable behaviour from Hillyard, she felt more confident than usual, and looked forward to an increasing understanding between herself and her husband.

As the men drank their after-dinner port, Donald noticed that Hillyard was drinking heavily and had sunk into a gloomy silence, disregarding all attempts by the others to bring him into the conversation. Donald knew that many, perhaps all, of the men present knew about the words exchanged in court that morning, and he felt the tension rising, as Hillyard's behaviour became increasingly boorish. The only speech anyone had managed to get out of him since the ladies retired had been, 'Pass the port,' uttered in an increasingly peremptory voice.

Donald's friend Martin Carr, who was sitting next to him, spoke in a low voice. 'I think we'd better get him back among the women,' he said, nodding towards Walter Hillyard. 'If his wife is present he won't make any trouble.'

'I think you're right,' agreed Donald. He stood up and said, 'Shall we join the ladies?'

'Ladies!' snorted Hillyard. 'They're not all ladies in your drawing room.' He stood up and glared steadily at his host. 'I know one that's no lady. And I wonder what sort of a man it is, that would marry a woman with a reputation like that.' He kept his eyes fixed on Donald, challenging him.

Before Donald had thought of how best he could reply to this attack most of the other men in the room had gathered round Hillyard and were trying to persuade him to leave the room. 'No, I won't go till I've had my say,' he shouted. 'You're all accomplices, that's what you are. Some of you knew about it even before the marriage, and all of you know about it now, I'll be bound. Perhaps the only one who doesn't know is the poor idiot himself. Perhaps nobody's had the courage to tell him, so I'll do it myself. Incest,' he roared, 'that's what it is. Did you never hear of the heavenly twins of Kintalloch?'

Donald turned to Martin. 'Get his wife. Tell her he's ill and must be taken home.'

The rest of the evening was not a success. Ellen realized that something more than a sudden indisposition on the part of one of the guests was involved, but had to pretend that nothing more serious had taken place.

As soon as the guests had left she turned to her husband, white-faced. 'What happened?'

'Oh, nothing. Hillyard drank too much and turned nasty. That's all.' And he turned on his heel and shut himself up in his bedroom.

Ellen was hurt and disappointed by his silence. Just when she thought that the incident with Hillyard was going to bring them closer together, it now seemed to be having the opposite effect. She knew from the constrained manner of all the other men that something pretty disagreeable had happened. It had obviously been quite a shock to Donald. Perhaps by tomorrow he would have settled down enough to be able to speak about it. But the next day came, and others followed, and Donald remained aloof. Even his interest in Meg seemed to wane for a while, but the child soon won him back to his usual complaisance with her.

As time passed and the situation didn't improve Ellen found herself worrying more and more about it. She had never known whether Donald had ever heard anything about her relationship with her brother, and the rumours that had circulated about this. If he had, he had evidently disbelieved them. Could it be that he had known nothing, and that Hillyard had said something out of spite? Or perhaps he had heard the rumours, had disbelieved them, and had now been told something more damaging? She could not bring herself to mention the subject to him. And anyway, what if it had nothing to do with that? She tormented herself over his silence for a long time, and in the end came to accept it. Her hope of a deeper understanding between them had

38

to be abandoned. It was, in a way, a reversal of their original roles. Now it was Donald who held aloof, as she had done till after the birth of their child. She told herself that it was only fair that she should have to take a taste of her own medicine. After all, it must have been much worse for Donald. At least, she told herself, I'm not in love with him. And I've got Meg. During those first years he had nothing to cover my silence with.

Donald spent a sleepless night, trying to dismiss the whole thing as malicious gossip, something Hillyard had invented just to hit back at him. He had never noticed any signs of unusual affection between Ellen and Tom; and indeed, ever since the ban on their sleeping together was imposed on their seventh birthday, they had always tried to appear as indifferent to each other as possible, at least in public, aware that there was some sort of shame attached to their love, without any idea, initially, of why this should be so. But their public indifference was belied by their tendency to sleep together whenever anything occurred to upset either of them – and, on occasion, guiltily, just for the sheer joy of being together. Sometimes their parents found out that they had not slept apart and chided them. Sometimes the servants found out and did not chide. But the word got round.

As he tried to puzzle out the truth of the situation Donald came to the conclusion that he would surely have heard something during the years that he had been frequenting Kintalloch. Then it occurred to him that he was only there at weekends, and always in the company of at least one of the Lindsays. Obviously no one was going to raise the subject in their presence. But a guilty secret of this kind might be the explanation of Ellen's silence and lack of response. After brooding over this possibility for some time, he was struck by another thought. Supposing she had heard these rumours and was innocent – would this not also be an explanation of her distant manner? How would you expect a young woman to react under such an accusation? Might it even be that this was what had prompted her to decide on leaving Kintalloch in the first place?

39

So Donald's thoughts went backwards and forwards all night like a shuttlecock, at one moment convinced of Ellen's guilt, at the next shuddering away from such a possibility, to a conviction of her innocence. He tried to persuade himself that the whole thing was a fabrication of Hillyard's. But what about the reaction of the others? Would they have been so discountenanced if there had been no truth in the accusation? He was determined to get to the bottom of the matter. He couldn't possibly ask Ellen, of course. If she was guilty she would almost certainly not tell him the truth. If she was innocent, it would be unspeakable to burden her with such an accusation, just to put his mind at rest. No, he must find out from some other source.

Next morning, ignoring the fact that he had work to do in his office, he went to see Martin Carr.

'Martin, I know you'll tell me the truth. Am I to believe this accusation of Hillyard's?'

Martin looked down at the pen he held in his hand, then shook his head. 'I don't know, Donald. I really don't know.'

'But you'd heard something, some rumour?'

Martin sighed. 'Yes, I'd heard.'

'What?'

'Precisely what Hillyard said last night.'

'And when? Did you know about this before I married?'

'No. It was shortly after the wedding that I heard the rumour. Too late to do anything about it then. I thought the best thing was to keep silent.'

Martin was not quite truthful in his reply. He had in fact heard about the alleged incest two days before the wedding, and had been in a great quandary as to whether to tell Donald or not. In the end either prudence or cowardice kept him silent – he was never able to determine which had been the motive. For a long time he worried about whether he had done the right thing, especially every time that a new source brought the same breath of scandal to him. But as time went by and the marriage appeared to be a success, and when he saw how happy both parents were with their little girl, he decided he must have done the right thing, and dismissed the matter from his mind.

'I want to know your source.'

If only you knew how many sources, thought Martin.

'What's the point?' he said. 'You're not going to expose yourself to the consequences of following this up, are you? What do you hope to gain? A certainty of your wife's guilt? For you know you can never be given a certainty of her innocence. Nobody can prove she's innocent. Or do you think you can stop the rumours? Any action on your part will do nothing but spread them all the faster.'

Donald reflected for some time. At last he said, 'Yes, I see your point. Just one more question. Do you believe all this yourself?'

'I didn't know what to believe at first. Remember I hardly knew Ellen at the time. Now I know her well, and I have no doubts whatever. I think the whole thing is an abominable calumny.'

Here again Martin fell rather short of the truth. He was not convinced of Ellen's innocence, or of her guilt either, for that matter. He just didn't know. But he felt sure that the only positive thing to be done was to restore Donald's faith in his wife. 'Obviously,' he went on, 'you can't say anything to Ellen about it. You can't risk asking an innocent woman whether she's had an incestuous relationship with her brother. You'll just have to dismiss the matter from your mind. I know that's easier said than done. But that's what you've got to do. There's no other way.'

Donald sighed. 'I suppose you're right.' Then he burst out, 'But you're asking the impossible! How can I dismiss the matter from my mind? Could you?'

'Perhaps not. But I'd certainly try. And that's what you must do.'

Donald tried. But his thoughts kept hurrying back to the same bitter problem as soon as his mind had a free moment. He tried to occupy himself as much as possible. At first it was with work. But even the most fascinating points of law seemed to have lost some of their edge. Gradually he took to going out in the evenings again – with Martin, then with other friends. Finally he went back to his earlier habits and started having the odd, discreet affair. He justified this to himself by the argument that, whether Ellen was guilty or innocent, his suffering remained the same, because there was no way he could ever know. No amount of assurances, from Ellen, from Tom, or from anyone else, could ever prove anything, one way or the other. And since this irremovable doubt had estranged them, he was entitled to take what consolation he could. He often wondered whether Ellen knew of the rumours. If only she had told him! If only someone had told him! But he realized it would have been too much to expect Ellen to broach the subject, even if she were innocent.

Or perhaps more especially if she were innocent.

He suffered too on her account. She must feel the estrangement between them, and wonder about it. Her distress was something that must grieve them both. And yet he could do nothing about it. The subject was, and must for ever remain, tabu. Only if he had been convinced of her guilt would it have been possible to raise the subject with her. But as long as there was any possibility of her innocence, then he simply could not speak of the matter.

The only way he could cope with the situation was by distancing himself as much as possible from his home. This meant a reduction of the fairly frequent entertaining they had indulged in up till then. This, at least, lightened the social burden for Ellen. As for Donald, he felt he could no longer enjoy his position as host after that disastrous dinner party. The fear of another incident like the one provoked by Hillyard would have haunted him all the time.

6

The Crombies were in the habit of spending a few weeks at Kintalloch every summer, and a week or two at Christmas and Easter. Meg adored all her relations there – her two cousins, Gavin and Angus, both a little older than she was, Uncle Tom, serious and friendly, Aunt Bessie, always full of fun and more maternal than her own mother. For Meg, brought up as a rather solitary only child, always in adult company, the presence of her two little companions was a guarantee of utter bliss.

Everything about Kintalloch had a magical quality about it, and when she grew old enough to appreciate her mother's devotion to the place it seemed to her the most natural thing in the world. For Donald too, Kintalloch had always seemed a hallowed place. He had been brought up in the city and had no experience of country life till he started going to visit the Lindsays, and for him it was a revelation. Not that he would have traded his city life, with all its stimulation and satisfactions, for a permanent residence in the country. But Kintalloch was a wonderful haven, and he was glad that his daughter should be able to enjoy the magic, idyllic hours of country life that his childhood had lacked.

On the first visit to Kintalloch after Hillyard's explosion Donald wondered how he should react to Tom's presence and to seeing him and Ellen together. He had often wondered whether he should ask Tom about the rumours. After all, they had been friends for a long time, even before they were linked by marriage. But he realized that, whatever the truth might be, Tom would have to reject the accusation. What else could he do? At all costs he had to protect his sister's name. As to raising the subject with Bessie, that was even more unthinkable, and equally pointless. He liked Bessie, and valued her sense of fun as an antidote to the sterner view of life that all the Lindsay family seemed to possess, and he could discuss many things with her. But not this.

Ellen had to spend a certain amount of her time at Kintalloch in the lodge with her mother. Catherine led a quiet life, engrossed in her domestic tasks and her memories of the past, and seldom joined the others at the big house.

On one of these occasions Tom and Bessie and Donald had gone out for a walk with the three children. After a time Bessie announced it was time for her to go back, and asked Donald to accompany her. As soon as they were out of hearing she tackled him.

'What's bothering you, Donald?' she asked bluntly.

'What do you mean, what's bothering me?'

'You know very well what I mean. I can see it, Tom can see it, even Meg has been telling us that something is making her father very sad. What is it?'

'Oh, nothing. Nothing worth talking about, anyway.'

'Everything's worth talking about. Especially the things that upset us.'

'I expect you're right. In general terms, that is. But there are some things, some special circumstances . . . '

After a moment's silence Bessie remarked, 'I suppose you must have heard the rumours. I'm surprised it hasn't happened before.'

'What rumours?' He couldn't believe that Bessie was actually proposing to discuss her husband's possible incest. But what else could she mean?

'The rumours about Tom and Ellen. Is that it?'

He nodded. After a pause he said, 'So you've heard them too?'

'Yes, of course. It's all over the village. Has been for years.'

He sighed. 'Well, I only wish I'd heard them years ago.'

'And you wouldn't have married Ellen?'

'That follows, doesn't it?'

'Why does it?'

'Well, would you have married Tom if you'd known?'

'I did know.'

'You knew *before* you married him?' Donald sounded incredulous.

'Yes, from the very start.'

He thought this over for a while, then said:

'You must have been terribly in love with him to accept him, knowing that.'

Bessie laughed. 'No, I wasn't at all in love with him when I accepted him. That came later.'

'I don't seem to know as much about human nature as I thought I did,' remarked Donald. 'I thought you seemed very much in love with him when you married.'

'I was, by that time. It doesn't take long, you know. Especially when a man like Tom comes wooing you. You fall in love out of sheer gratitude. As it happens I'd already decided I'd rather like to be mistress of Kintalloch. I know that sounds a bit mercenary, but I was only a girl, and it seemed rather a jolly prospect. And then when he fell in with my plans, as it were, and when I got to know him better and saw what sort of a man he was, I just couldn't believe my luck. I still can't believe it.'

'In spite of the scandal?'

'In spite of the scandal. I'm not inclined to think ill of people in general, and I decided from the start that I wasn't going to believe any of it.'

'And you still don't?'

Bessie was silent a moment. 'I'm almost certain that it's not true. Almost.'

'And you've never spoken about it with Tom?'

'Never.'

'Nor to Ellen?'

'Good heavens, no. If I couldn't even approach Tom about it . . . '

'And he's a lot more approachable than Ellen, you mean? Yes,

I can see that. So I presume you don't know whether he knows that you know?'

Bessie shocked him by bursting out laughing. 'Oh, dear. It does sound so funny, when you put it that way. All this knowing about knowing about knowing. I'm sorry, you must think I'm incurably flippant. I can see that it's a lot worse for you – the not knowing, I mean. You're a man who likes to know. By nature and by profession, I suppose. I'm just a very everyday sort of person. I take life as it comes. I'm not prepared to torture myself about something that just might be the case. I'm more interested in the things I do know. And I know that Tom's a wonderful husband, and an excellent father, and that as long as he's alive Kintalloch is in good hands. Can't you take comfort from the fact that Ellen has been a good wife to you, and is an excellent mother? Isn't that enough?'

'Oh, Bessie, I wish I were like you. I wish I could say yes, that's enough. But I just can't shut my eyes to this shadow hanging over everything. I can't shut my eyes to the fact that wherever I go people may be whispering things behind my back.' Suddenly Donald turned towards her, almost violently:

'My God, woman, have you no pride?'

'Not that kind,' was her reply.

7

'Meg!' Ellen called to her daughter from the foot of the stairs.

'Yes, Mother?' Meg leaned over the balustrade, two floors up.

'That's Miss Hamilton on her way now. You'd better go to the school room and be ready for her.'

'Yes, Mother.'

Meg went back into her bedroom, put away her book and tidied her hair. She knew she had plenty of time while the usual ceremonies were being performed downstairs. And anyway Miss Hamilton always took her time on the stairs. Not through shortness of breath or any other physical disability, but on principle. A lady never hurries.

The elaborate morning ritual was part of Ellen's survival plan. She had managed to get through the ordeal of receiving her daughter's governess on the first occasion a few years ago, and had turned that into a model for all future occasions. She had never really felt at ease in the life that marriage to Donald had forced upon her. Whenever she found a manageable way of coping with any of her duties she tended to crystallize the pattern of events into a set formula, to be followed religiously from then on. She felt she could only relax in the security of a completely familiar situation. Miss Hamilton had taken her cue from her new employer, and never disconcerted her by any impromptu deviations from the norm.

Ellen often wondered whether this acquiescence was due simply to a desire to please her employer or to a personal liking for the predictable and ceremonious. A governess, after all, could be forgiven for feeling on shaky ground in certain circumstances. It was natural that she should appreciate a clear demarcation of roles, a well-learned script. It was she, Ellen, who had little excuse for the unease she habitually felt in the presence of strangers – and the term 'strangers' included more or less everyone except her own immediate family circle.

So she stood at the window every morning, on the lookout for the tall spare figure. Miss Hamilton's punctuality was a great help in this matter. Ellen knew to the nearest half minute at what time to take up her post. As soon as the governess was sighted Ellen would call to Meg, then go back to the drawing room and take up her position beside the elaborate bird-cage. She was always engaged in feeding the bird when Miss Hamilton was announced.

And it was not by pure chance that she had been feeding the canary on Miss Hamilton's first visit. She had been much exercised by the problem of whether she should receive the governess standing or sitting. She had meant to ask Donald, but he had left the house earlier than usual that day, before she had been able to tackle him on the matter. You don't stand up for a servant, she told herself. But then, a governess? Not quite a servant, is she, even if you are employing her. And she knew that this particular governess came from a very good family. The Hamiltons had belonged to a social set at least as good as their own. Desperately she had cast about in her mind for some sort of activity that called for a standing position. Just then the canary had burst into song. Eureka! That was the answer.

Gratefully she moved over to the little creature, and was busy pouring out some more seeds for it when Miss Hamilton was announced.

On this particular morning there was regret mixed with the gratitude that the recollection of that first day usually evoked, for earlier that morning she had found the bird lying dead in its cage. Now she stood uncertain, doubly at a loss. Any change in her routine disconcerted her, and this change brought with it a renewed need for a decision. Perhaps the best thing would be just to stand at the window, as if examining the weather. If this arrangement seemed to work all right, then the stance could be incorporated into the normal routine.

Miss Hamilton did not permit herself any remark on the new situation. But Ellen noticed her initial movement in the direction of the bird-cage.

'Yes, Miss Hamilton,' she said, 'I'm afraid we have sustained a loss.'

Miss Hamilton sympathized, and hoped it had not been too great a blow to her pupil.

'She was fond of the little creature,' Ellen said. 'But she is after all fourteen years old, and has to accept the fact that loss of one kind or another is a part of life. Some of us have to accept this even earlier. I don't think you'll find her too upset.'

When she entered the school room Miss Hamilton judged that Meg looked composed enough to speak about the death. '*Passer mortuus est,*' she quoted.

The girl's eyes flashed in outrage. 'But it wasn't a *sparrow*,' she cried, 'it was a *canary*.'

'I quote, my dear, I quote. *Passer mortuus est meae puellae.* Catullus. One of the great Latin poets. But not entirely suitable for a young lady.'

Meg had resumed her usual subdued manner.

'Did he write about birds?' she enquired.

Miss Hamilton's eyelids did not flicker. 'He wrote about love. And about not wasting time. *Vivamus mea Lesbia atque amemus.* So we had better heed that part of his message, *mutatis mutandis*, and make a start on today's lessons.'

She realized Meg must be a bit upset after all. The outburst about the canary was not typical of her. A pity, she thought. The mention of Catullus would have been a good opportunity to introduce the subject of love poetry. She was constantly aware of the fact that her approach to teaching might perhaps be rather Victorian, or at least Edwardian. This was, after all, 1914. And she felt it was up to her to give the girl as wide an outlook as possible.

Miss Hamilton liked her employers, but feared that with so withdrawn a mother Meg stood little chance of finding out about the world at large. She could hardly regret the decision to educate Meg at home, and realized it was a natural one for such a mother to make. She also felt pretty certain that it was at Mrs Crombie's wish that she had been asked to come and teach Meg daily, rather than live in the house with the family. Mrs Crombie liked as few people about the house as possible. Miss Hamilton respected this wish and found it perfectly natural in one so shy; but she was aware that this state of affairs imposed a strange isolation on the girl. Mr Crombie too was a well-educated man, and in that sense a good companion for Meg. But he seemed to spend little time in the house. Most of the time Meg was with her mother or her governess. So she felt some concern for the girl, and a great sense of responsibility. Meg seemed happy enough, but lamentably ill prepared for a normal adult life.

It was just as well that she spent her holidays with her parents at the mother's family home, Kintalloch. There at least she had the company of her cousins. Miss Hamilton remembered her own happy childhood with brothers and sisters, school friends and neighbours' children. How sad to be deprived of all this enjoyment and all this learning! And what a handicap it must be in later life! She felt more affection for Meg than she had ever felt for any of her other pupils, but the affection was tinged with concern for this quiet, intelligent, yet tentative girl. Not that she looked as ill at ease in her world as her mother did. But she did rather give the impression of being a visitor to the planet. She certainly didn't look like a girl who has taken possession of her life.

'She hasn't found her centre,' were the words with which Miss Hamilton summed up the situation to herself.

8

It was not long after the canary's death that Miss Hamilton decided that the time was ripe to ask Mrs Crombie whether she could be permitted to invite Meg to her house for tea some afternoon. Ellen considered the matter and came up with her usual solution to the unscheduled. She would ask her husband. Mr Crombie saw no objection, so the invitation was officially issued and ceremoniously accepted. For Meg it was an exciting occasion. An outing of any sort was a landmark in her quiet life; and she had often wondered about Miss Hamilton's private life. She knew she must be hard up – why else would anyone become a governess? Besides, she always seemed to wear the same clothes. And she always came and went on foot. Was this to save money? When asked how long it took her she always replied vaguely:

'Oh, about half an hour.'

It was with some excitement that Meg set off in her mother's company on the agreed day. Ellen was to accompany her to the house and leave her there, to be collected by her father a couple of hours later. For the first time she was to make a social call on her own. She had been delivered and collected before, but only to one or other of the few children's parties that had come her way. This was a very different matter.

Meg felt both elated and apprehensive as they set out. Miss Hamilton lived in an area of modest gentility in the south of Edinburgh. In order to get there they had to take a tramcar into the centre of the town, and then change. A two-tram journey was something quite out of the ordinary for Meg, and she enjoyed every swaying minute.

'It's a terribly long journey, isn't it, Mama? How on earth does Miss Hamilton manage it on foot twice a day?'

Ellen thought the matter over, then said, 'She's obviously a strong, healthy woman. Besides, walking is good for you.'

'Well, why didn't we walk?'

'Oh, my dear!' Ellen sounded shocked. 'It's much too far.'

'Not for Miss Hamilton. And she isn't even a countrywoman, like you.'

'I'm hardly that now. It's many years since I lived in the country.' And the habitual look of regret on Ellen's face deepened to one of real sadness.

Meg gave her mother's arm a squeeze. 'Never mind, Mama,' she said. 'It will soon be summer and we'll all go to Kintalloch and see Uncle Tom and Aunt Bessie.'

'Yes, dear,' her mother agreed. 'We'll all go to Kintalloch and see Uncle Tom – and Aunt Bessie.'

Miss Hamilton's house turned out to be in a row of tiny, neat little terraced houses, each with a minute garden in front of it. Some had a rather forlorn appearance, but Miss Hamilton's house was trim and well cared for, and the little garden was full of flowers.

As they stood on the doorstep Meg thought of the big, well kept gardens that their house in the New Town looked out to, and her mother's thoughts had flown to the fields and moors round Kintalloch.

It was Miss Hamilton herself who opened the door. Ellen declined the invitation to come in. No, she had things to do in town. After the necessary civilities she left, and Meg was ushered into a compressed sitting room. After a quarter of an hour's rather forced conversation Miss Hamilton disappeared to get the tea.

Meg spent the time examining the many photographs with which the room was decorated. There was one of a splendid Victorian villa with an equally splendid Victorian family ranged before the steps. She was looking at this when Miss Hamilton came in with the tea-tray.

'Is this one of the families you've been with, Miss Hamilton?' she asked.

'No, dear, that's my own family. We were quite a crowd, weren't we?'

Meg was struck by the disparity between the family seat and the present home of one of its members. She longed to ask questions, but was afraid this might be considered rude.

Miss Hamilton saw the thoughtful look on the girl's face, and wondered whether she should speak of herself and her family. For a long time now she had been torn between fear of overstepping the limits laid down by society for the amount of personal explanation permitted to governesses, and a desire to speak more freely with the girl, of whom she had grown extremely fond, and whose affection she felt she had won. Perhaps now, when there could be no suggestion that the time should be spent on school subjects, she might be allowed to talk about herself and her home.

It was Meg who solved the problem, by asking:

'What made you become a governess, Miss Hamilton?' As soon as she had asked the question she was covered with confusion. She hadn't meant to ask it, as she was afraid it might cause offence, and yet, without knowing why, she had done so.

'Sheer necessity, my dear,' came the reply. 'Shall I tell you about it?'

'Oh, yes. Please.' Meg gave a sigh of relief. Her impromptu question had not given offence. In fact, she got the impression that Miss Hamilton was eager to talk about herself and her family. And Meg was only too glad to listen.

'Well, as you can see, we were all pretty comfortably off. We were a large family and a happy one. The only problem was that my papa had not much of what you would call a head for business. He tended to leave things in other people's hands as much as possible. When he realized that things weren't going well he was inclined to hope, like Mr Micawber . . . '

'That something would turn up?' suggested Meg, taking her cue from the familiar pause which meant that Miss Hamilton was waiting for a reference to be recognized.

'Exactly. And nothing did turn up. At least, nothing positive. And then suddenly, with incredible speed, the end came. Papa had absolutely nothing left. I don't know how these things happen, but they do. I expect your papa comes across this sort of thing in his work. We had to give up the house and the servants. Those of us who were old enough to work had to find something right away. As a well brought up young lady, the only thing I could possibly do was help to fashion other well brought up young ladies. And that's what I've been doing ever since.'

Meg examined the photograph again. 'Is that you there?' she asked, pointing to the tallest of the young women. On seeing her governess nod, she exclaimed:

'Oh, you were beautiful, weren't you?' Then she blushed suddenly, as she realized the implications of the past tense.

Miss Hamilton laughed. 'After a certain age no woman can *expect* to retain her beauty. A very few do. Your mama is one of the fortunate exceptions. And you're very like her. You may have the same good fortune.'

Meg blushed again, this time with pleasure. To be told she was like her beautiful mother was always a joy to her. This was one of the things that adult life seemed to promise her – to be lovely and admired for her beauty, like her mother. In the midst of her pleasure and embarrassment it occurred to her that even now Miss Hamilton had a certain elegance and an undeniable air of distinction. You couldn't compare her with Mama, but sometimes, especially today, she really looked quite attractive. She would have liked to tell her so, but was held back by the awkwardness of youth, and at the same time by a sensitivity that told her that a compliment just now, so soon after having implied that all her beauty was gone, might be taken as a tardy attempt at reparation, rather than the expression of a sincere opinion.

Instead she changed the subject.

'How nice it must be, to have so many brothers and sisters.'

'Yes, it was lovely. We had a wonderful childhood. Papa taught us at home. I don't know how he had the patience to teach so many of us, all at different stages. He must have been an exceptional teacher.'

Now Meg had the courage to risk a compliment, knowing that the recipient would realize that this one at least was heartfelt. 'Like his daughter,' she said.

Miss Hamilton gave a delighted laugh.

'I've been lucky,' she said. 'No unteachable pupils.'

Meg was enjoying herself so much that she could hardly believe it was her father come to collect her when they heard the doorbell ring.

'Oh, Papa! It can't possibly be time to go yet,' she exclaimed as he came in.

Donald had intended to call for his daughter without going into the house. He was never able to decide what had made him change his mind. It must have been something about Miss Hamilton's appearance. He seldom came across her in the daily routine, and it now struck him that she looked smarter and younger than he remembered her, and livelier and brighter as well. In short, she looked like a woman who was enjoying herself thoroughly. Donald had allowed himself to accept her invitation to come in, and then to let her make another pot of tea.

'And that will be an excuse for Meg and me to start all over again, won't it?' she had suggested, laughing.

Meg agreed, laughing too.

While Miss Hamilton was in the kitchen Meg pointed out the family photograph.

'Did you know she came from that sort of family?' she asked.

'Yes, my dear. One doesn't engage a governess without finding out a great deal about her.'

Just then Miss Hamilton came back into the room, and Donald leapt up to help her with the tea things. Conversation flowed easily, mainly between the two adults, though occasionally Meg ventured to join in. She was pleased to see how well her father and her governess were getting on. The sparkle in Miss Hamilton's manner that had delighted her in the course of their conversation now seemed to have spread to her father. Papa, she knew, could be wonderfully witty and entertaining, although this aspect of him was seldom to the fore. But now he and Miss Hamilton seemed to spark each other off. They joked and laughed and quoted Latin tags and French proverbs and lines of English poetry. As she ate yet another cream cake Meg felt she was having a double feast. How wonderful it would be when she was grown up and could talk like that too!

When her father said, 'Well, Meg, *tempus fugit*, it's time we went home,' Meg pleaded for another few minutes.

'It's so lovely here,' she exclaimed, her eyes shining as she looked round the small, crowded room.

'Yes dear. But your mama awaits, and we've already taken up too much of Miss Hamilton's time. We really must go.'

Meg stood up, sighing. *'C'est la vie,'* she conceded, and felt that she had risen to the level of the adults.

On their way home she was enthusiastic about the visit. 'I never thought I'd enjoy it *so* much. I hadn't realized what a wonderful person Miss Hamilton is. It's like seeing her in quite a different light, isn't it?'

Her father agreed. He too felt he had seen the governess in quite a different light.

As she began to clear away the tea things Miss Hamilton felt very happy about the way the visit had gone. Meg had relaxed and blossomed even more than she had hoped for, and she felt that their relationship had widened and deepened. She really is a darling, she thought. Then she thought of the father, and stood a long time gazing abstractedly out of the window, holding the tea tray in her hands. Finally she gave an odd little smile, sighed, and said 'I wonder,' as she turned to go out of the room.

She felt so convinced that she had made an impression on the father that she would not have been at all surprised if he had made some excuse or other for turning up in the school room during the lessons some day.

But the days went past and the weeks went past, and Miss Hamilton decided she must have been wrong. Just as well, she thought, not without a tinge of regret, it would only have complicated matters. My commitment is to Meg, and that must come first.

Nearly two months after the tea party, on her way home after the day's lessons, Miss Hamilton rounded a corner and found Donald Crombie approaching her. At first she thought the meeting was due to pure chance; but after a moment's casual conversation he asked her to allow him to accompany her part of the way, and the certainty she had felt before returned. The conversation was less lively than during their previous meeting. And yet Donald stayed beside her while they persevered with a variety of subjects that at that moment were supremely unimportant to both of them.

When they got to her house she stopped at the gate and held out her hand. 'Well, as you know, Mr Crombie, this is where I live. I must thank you for the pleasure of your company during my long walk.'

Donald bowed and took her hand. He held it rather longer than was usual for a polite farewell handshake. Then, still holding her hand, and looking at her with a serious expression, he asked:

'May I come in? I should very much like to talk to you.'

She hesitated. 'Perhaps some other time,' she suggested at last. 'With Meg, perhaps?'

He shook his head. 'No, Miss Hamilton, not with Meg. Please,' he pleaded, 'it's very important.' And he opened the garden gate for her.

Donald found it rather hard to proceed once they were in the house. What he wanted was to propose an illicit liaison. It was, after all, the only thing he had to offer. There could be no question of any other, socially acceptable, relationship between them. And yet, in spite of his ready tongue and his experience, he felt slightly daunted by this tall, composed woman. They sat in the chairs they had occupied during his previous visit, and looked at each other guardedly. Miss Hamilton felt sure she perfectly understood the purpose of his visit, and was wondering in what terms he would broach the subject.

Donald, who had been rehearsing this meeting for some weeks, simply couldn't get started on any of the lines of approach that had seemed so promising in his imaginary conversations. Suddenly he was reminded of his frustrated attempt at making a formal proposal to Ellen. For a few seconds he thought he was going to burst out laughing. It's too ridiculous, he thought. I have a fine command of language in court. I have no difficulty at all in setting up a flirtatious conversation with most women. And yet, when it really matters . . .

Miss Hamilton was looking at him with just a touch of irony in her expression. In the end she came to his rescue.

'You said, Mr Crombie, that you did not wish Meg to be present. Am I to infer from this that you wish to speak to me about Meg? Or not?'

'No, not about Meg.'

'Well, that at any rate reduces the range of possibilities,' she remarked. 'But it still leaves rather a wide field. Could you perhaps tell me what it is you wish to speak to me about?'

Donald told her. Haltingly at first, then with more confidence, he spoke of the enormous impression she had made on him during his earlier visit. Soon he felt his rhetoric was flowing nicely. He paused when he came to the end of his exposition, before embarking on any constructive suggestion.

At that point Miss Hamilton intervened.

'Well, Mr Crombie,' she said, 'I must admit to feeling extremely flattered by all you have said.' She stood up. 'Now it but remains for me to thank you for your undeservedly high opinion of me. And that, I think, is the matter concluded.'

She looked so majestic, standing there in front of him (for he had been too taken aback to stand up when she did), that he nearly accepted his dismissal. But he was not in the habit of failing in this sort of enterprise, and the thought of being turned down by a governess goaded him into action. He spoke again, eloquently, pleading his cause.

She listened in silence, then said:

'And what about Meg?'

'Meg? What about her? It has nothing to do with Meg.'

'I think it has a great deal to do with Meg.'

'In what way?'

'You realize I cannot possibly go on teaching her while indulging in clandestine meetings with her father. For you know very well that any relationship between us must be clandestine.'

'Yes,' he said, 'I fully realize that, while regretting it deeply. But as for Meg, she need never know. In fact, I should say she ought to be the last person to know.'

'Or the second-last?' suggested Miss Hamilton.

Donald gave a little snort of impatience. 'You're making things difficult for me, aren't you?'

'I'm only trying to be realistic.'

'So am I. And I still fail to see what it's got to do with Meg.'

'In that case, Mr Crombie, it's evident that you have no conception of what it is to be a teacher. One of the essentials of good teaching is a foundation of mutual respect and trust. I cannot possibly betray that trust and go on teaching Meg at the same time.'

'In other words, you consider you have to make a choice between us?'

She nodded.

'And you choose Meg?' he continued.

'Yes, I choose Meg. I should hope that, in similar circumstances, I should always choose the pupil. And when the pupil is Meg there can be no hesitation. She is an exceptionally lovable girl, and a rather vulnerable one as yet. I think she needs the help of a governess. And I think that a change of teacher at this point would have a damaging effect on her. She is very sensitive, very uncertain.'

Donald left feeling angry, disappointed, and extremely foolish. To be rejected in favour of one's daughter was an unexpected turn of events.

After he had gone Miss Hamilton wandered about the house restlessly. At the beginning of the interview she had been if anything rather amused. Then, when the conversation turned on Meg, she had felt herself fully committed to her role as teacher. But now she was aware that all her buoyancy and exaltation were draining out of her. All she could think of now was the tantalising thought of what might have been. She found Donald Crombie immensely attractive, and it was obvious that the attraction was mutual. She felt sure that they could have been very happy together. In spite of her reluctance to enter into an illicit relationship she was convinced that she would have done so, had he not been Meg's father. This was not the first time in her life that she had felt obliged to renounce the promise of happiness. She spent the evening trying to occupy herself, trying to take her mind off past unhappiness and present frustration. In the end she went to bed early and allowed herself the rare indulgence of tears.

9

The first two years of the war made little impact on the Crombie and Lindsay families. Tom's boys, Gavin and Angus, were too young for active service, and daily life was not seriously affected for any of them. There was the general worry and concern over what was happening at the front, and sadness at the ever-increasing number of casualties. But ordinary life went on, till one day in 1916, when Ellen got a letter from Tom telling her that Gavin was now in the army, and expected to be sent to France in the near future. It was shortly before their usual summer holiday in Kintalloch, and Meg was stunned by the realization that one of her loved companions would no longer be with them. Only a few months ago, on their last visit, he had still been one of them, one of 'the children'; and now he was virtually on his way to the trenches. She felt she was suddenly standing on the brink of the grown-up world. It was a little frightening, and at the same time exciting and immensely interesting.

A few days later Gavin called to say goodbye. He was to take the train south that very day, and had already parted from his parents and Kintalloch. Seeing him in his uniform brought home to Meg the differences between them. His place was in the officers' mess, hers was still in the school room. In view of his total elevation to adult life, Meg felt honoured when he suggested that they should go for a walk together.

'Which way?' she asked, as they stepped out of the house.

'Any way, as long as it takes us to the old part of the town. There's not much point in walking about the New Town, is there?'

'Why ever not?' she cried in astonishment.

'Well, it's all the same, isn't it? Terribly monotonous.'

Meg looked at him in amazement. She had always been given

to understand that she was very lucky to live in the New Town, by far the best part of Edinburgh, and had accordingly enjoyed walking along its elegant streets. Seeing her look of surprise and dismay, Gavin realized he had said the wrong thing. Instead of dismissing the matter from his mind, he felt impelled to justify his view, precisely because her opinion mattered so much to him:

'I mean, the houses are all exactly alike, aren't they?'

'And why shouldn't they be? They're beautiful, isn't that enough?'

'No, I want diversity as well as beauty. You don't get rows and rows of the same house repeated again and again in the country.'

'No, you get rows and rows of exactly the same tree!'

'I can see you've never really looked at trees,' he replied. 'You'll never get two alike. Never. Each is an individual, and that's more than you can say about the houses in this part of the town.'

Suddenly Meg realized that soon he would be hundreds of miles away, in a different and dangerous life, and she wondered what on earth they were doing, arguing about trees and houses. She put her hand through his arm and said, 'Let's go to the Royal Mile. Is that old and irregular enough for you?'

He smiled. 'Yes, that will do nicely.'

He too had been asking himself why on earth he was arguing with her, today of all days, and was relieved and grateful to her for ending their little difference. As far back as he could remember he had hoped that one day he would marry Meg. He loved her gentleness and sweetness of character, her devotion to Kintalloch, and the way she looked up to him as the big cousin who knew everything and could do everything. This latter aspect was founded mainly on the fact that when they were together they were nearly always on his territory. As the elder of the two brothers he was used to leading; and Meg, brought up among adults, was used to being led. They fell into their roles naturally and harmoniously. To Gavin it seemed desirable and right that the relationship should develop into that of man and wife. But the war had come too soon for them. Meg was only sixteen. How could he ask her to make any promise to him at this stage? And yet he longed to be able to go away with the assurance from her that she would wait for him.

They spent all afternoon wandering about the old part of the town, talking happily, with no recurrence of their earlier disagreement. But all the time the struggle was going on in Gavin's mind. His conviction that it would not be fair to raise the subject fought with his need for reassurance in the face of the unknown dangers ahead of him.

When they got back to the house it was nearly time for him to go for his train. He refused to go in with her, saying it really was getting late. He hung back for a moment, then said:

'Look, Meg, there's something I want to say, only I don't really know if I should. It's just that . . . if you would be prepared to wait . . . '

'I hate waiting!' Meg broke out almost petulantly, quite unaware of the direction the conversation was meant to take. Then, seeing the look of deep despondency that her outburst had brought to Gavin's face, she added with her usual gentleness:

'I'm sorry, Gavin, that was a selfish thing to say. It's just that all my life seems to be nothing but waiting. "Wait till you're older, wait till Papa comes, wait till you're grown up," and so on. But I shouldn't have interrupted. Please go on.'

This apology underlined Meg's youthfulness, but at the same time it brought some comfort to Gavin. Perhaps she hadn't realized what he meant, perhaps she hadn't rejected him outright.

'It's just,' he faltered, 'it's just that, when I come back, if I come back . . . '

'Oh, Gavin!' she exclaimed, looking up at him in deep dismay, while tears flooded into her eyes, 'don't say *if*. Oh, don't say it. You *must* come back!'

Gavin looked at the tears in her eyes and heaved a great sigh of relief. Thank God, he thought, she cares, she really does care. I don't think she knows what we're talking about, but it doesn't matter. She doesn't despise me, she's not indifferent.

'I'll come back, Meg,' he said. Then he took her hand, kissed it, and walked quickly away.

Meg went into the house, closed the door, and leaned against it. An immense new possibility had suddenly entered her world. I think, she said to herself, I think I've just had my first proposal. She went upstairs thoughtfully, wondering whether she'd accepted it.

A few days later one of the maids came to tell her that her presence was required in the library.

'My father?' asked Meg.

'Both of 'em,' replied the maid, sensing something beyond the ordinary run of things.

'Oh!'

Meg was quite taken aback. It was most unusual for both parents to wish to speak to her together. The last time had been nearly a year ago, when Grandmother Catherine had been found dead in her bed one morning. She hoped no other calamity had befallen the family. Not Gavin, surely?

She hurried down anxiously and entered the room. Her father was sitting at his usual place at the desk, her mother on a hard-backed armchair near the window.

'Sit down, Margaret,' said her father.

Margaret! she thought. What have I done? Neither of her parents ever addressed her by her full name except in cases of serious misdemeanour. As she sat down she was unable to stifle a feeling of apprehension, in spite of her conviction that she had done nothing wrong.

She looked from one parent to the other, waiting for the silence to be broken.

'We wanted to speak to you about this letter. It's from Gavin.'

Meg felt a sudden rush of blood rising to her face. I must look like a beetroot, she thought. She didn't dare look up at either parent, but felt sure they were looking at her, and must have seen her blush.

'I suppose you have some idea of what the letter is about?' asked her father.

'No, none whatever,' she replied, mystified. And then it occurred to her that perhaps she *should* have some idea. She hung her head and murmured, 'Unless . . . unless it's . . . '

'Oh, read the letter to her, for goodness sake, Donald.' Her mother sounded just a little impatient.

'Very well.'

And Donald read out a brief statement of the fact that Gavin hoped to marry Meg, but realized she was too young to be tied as yet. All he wanted to know was whether Meg's parents would give their blessing to the marriage when the time came. That was all.

'Well, Margaret,' asked her father, 'did you know he was going to write?'

'No, I had no idea.'

'Had he said nothing to you about his feelings, his hopes?'

'No. Well, perhaps. Yes. I'm not sure.'

Her father was looking at her quizzically, leaving her to struggle on.

'What did he say, Meg?' The question came from her mother.

Meg took courage and said:

'He said something about waiting. But I didn't understand. Not till after he'd gone. And then I thought, perhaps . . . ' Her voice trailed off into silence.

There was a little gleam of amusement in her father's eyes.

'Well, come now, Meg. You can at least tell *us*. Did he propose to you, or not?'

'I don't know, really.' Meg felt somewhat reassured by the return to the usual form of her name, but she was still dubious as to what the situation really was. If she hadn't mismanaged the whole thing so badly she would have been able to give her parents a clear-cut answer. 'There was that bit about waiting. Was that a proposal, do you think?'

Donald was chuckling quietly to himself, and left Ellen to comment:

'I should think that was the intention. Proposals aren't always as precise and elegant as literature might lead you to expect.'

Donald's chuckle turned into a laugh. Then he said:

'I think you'd be safe in classifying the incident as a proposal. I'm not quite sure what a court of law would make of it, but for practical purposes you can consider yourself proposed to. Now, the next point to be elucidated is this: did you accept?'

Meg blushed again, this time with mortification. Not knowing whether she was engaged or not seemed a proof of her total ineptitude as an adult. She could find nothing to say.

'Well, young lady, does silence mean consent?' enquired her father. 'Did you say yes?'

Meg shook her head. 'No. But then, there was really nothing to say yes to, was there? At least, there may have been, but I didn't realize it at the time.'

'Well, what did you say?'

'I don't know. I really can't remember, I was so confused. And I didn't realize what he was talking about. But he said something about perhaps not coming back, from the war, I mean, and I said he *must* come back, and then he suddenly looked much happier and went away, saying he *would* come back, or something of the sort.' She couldn't bring herself to mention that he had kissed her hand. This was too precious and too private to share with anyone.

Ellen was smiling, and Donald was smiling too and shaking his head.

'I think we'll have to speak to Miss Hamilton about this,' he said in mock seriousness. 'The girl's obviously illiterate as far as the language of love is concerned.'

Meg burst into tears:

'I don't think it's at all funny,' she sobbed. 'I just wish someone would tell me – am I engaged or not?'

Donald remembered his own discomfiture during the ten minutes or so that the same question had perplexed him some twenty years before, and got up and put an arm round his daughter's shoulders. 'Only if that's what you want, my dear. It's your choice. And you've plenty of time to decide.'

Meg pointed out that this still didn't solve the problem of knowing whether Gavin considered she had pledged herself to him or not. In the end it was agreed that Donald should write back to the effect that he and Ellen would have no objection if Gavin were to pay his addresses to their daughter, when the time came. The next move would be up to him. It was just a question of waiting for him to write to her.

Meg decided she would just have to possess her soul in patience till his first letter arrived. That would surely make the situation clear.

But the weeks went past, and no letter came. Meg began to wonder whether she'd imagined the whole thing. Then she thought of Gavin's letter to her parents, and felt more reassured. But why didn't he write to *her*? Then Tom wrote to say that Gavin had been wounded shortly after his arrival at the front. He was now better, but still unable to use his right hand. This explained his silence. Meg felt sure he wouldn't want to have to get someone else to write that first letter to her. When at last the letter came it was clear that he did not think she had committed herself, but very much hoped she would do so in the near future. By this time Meg felt pretty certain that, as soon as her parents thought she was old enough, she would marry Gavin.

She often discussed the matter with her mother, who seemed less in favour of the marriage than Meg was. Not that Ellen raised any objections. But she just kept telling her that she must not hurry, that there was no need to make a decision just yet. Meg, however, kept on day-dreaming about the marriage, and dwelt at length on all the different advantages it offered.

'And Kintalloch, Mother, just think of it. Fancy being able to live at Kintalloch all the time. Wouldn't it be wonderful?'

'Yes, dear. But I suppose you and Gavin would live on one of the farms at first. You can't expect Uncle Tom and Aunt Bessie to move out just because you and Gavin want to move in. Or the lodge. You and Gavin might move into the lodge, now it's empty again.'

'Oh, that would be too small. The two of us couldn't possibly live there.'

'Two of us did,' replied her mother with a touch of asperity. 'Remember? I lived there with my mother till I got married.' Ellen wondered whether the comfort in which Meg had been brought up had perhaps given her rather unrealistic ideas. Besides, she would have liked a little more indication that Meg was marrying for love. But then, she reflected, she herself was hardly in a position to throw stones in this respect. She had married Donald purely out of a desire to escape from an unwelcome situation. She tried to steer the conversation towards an admission by Meg of her real feelings for Gavin.

Meg spoke with enthusiasm of Gavin and all his good qualities. 'We've always got on so well,' she said. 'He's like a big brother to me – with the added advantage that I can marry him, which I couldn't do if he really was my brother. But then, of course, I wouldn't want to, would I?'

Ellen didn't answer, and Meg looked at her enquiringly. Her mother was gazing out of the window, as if miles away. Oh, thought Meg, she's gone off on one of her absences again. She was used to a sudden loss of attention on the part of her mother, and had noticed the look of unhappiness that usually clouded her features at these times. She didn't know the cause of the sorrow, but felt it had something to do with Kintalloch. Was it a sort of permanent homesickness, she wondered? She could understand that. Kintalloch represented such total happiness for her that she was sure her mother must feel the same – more so, in fact, having been brought up there. She often wished she could do something to lift the veil of melancholy that seemed to hang permanently over her mother. Perhaps marrying Gavin would be the answer.

'And if I marry Gavin,' she went on, 'I'll be at Kintalloch all the time, and you'll be able to come as often as you like, and for as long as you like. Won't that be lovely?'

'Did you say *won't* or *wouldn't*? It's still supposed to be hypothetical, isn't it?'

'Yes, Mother, it is still hypothetical. I did say *won't*, but it was a hypothetical *won't*.'

Ellen smiled, but couldn't help wondering whether the hypothetical element in the situation wasn't gradually fading away.

As the weeks went past and Gavin's letters arrived it was clear that Meg considered herself engaged.

'Unofficially, of course,' she agreed. 'I know I'm too young, as yet.'

Donald seemed satisfied with the situation; but Ellen, in some obscure way, found it disquieting. She tried hard to find out why she didn't feel happy about the match. Gavin was a good, steady young man, and could give Meg just the right position in life. The thought of a closer bond with Kintalloch was also very tempting. And it was obviously Meg's own choice. No pressure had been put upon her. And yet, Ellen couldn't feel happy about it. Am I feeling perhaps just a little bit jealous? she asked herself. Here's Meg walking out of a happy childhood into what looks like an equally happy marriage. Am I jealous because it was all so different and difficult for me? Or am I just worried in case she's marrying too young, and doesn't really know her own mind? Does she really love him? Or is she perhaps swayed by the thought of giving me happiness by settling down in Kintalloch? Poor darling, if only she knew. Kintalloch is heaven to me, but it's a heaven with a bitter streak in it. I don't know if I could endure it much oftener than I do at present, and for longer visits.

Ellen's feelings for her brother had not changed over the years. She still wanted to be with him more than with anyone else on earth, her daughter included; but the joy of being with him was always clouded by the fact of Bessie's presence. Not just her presence; Bessie's mere existence marred for Ellen the happiness of being with Tom. The fact that Bessie seemed in all respects above reproach only made matters worse, by adding to Ellen's unhappiness a sense of her own injustice.

She worried over Meg's situation for months, then decided she must speak to Donald about it, difficult as she found it to discuss anything beyond the usual domestic trivia with him – partly because of her own natural reserve, and partly because of the continuing estrangement on his part that had begun many years ago. Anyway, it was a tricky question to approach. She could hardly make much of the fact that she didn't think Meg was really in love with Gavin, for Donald knew only too well that she herself had certainly not been in love with him when they married. Whether their own marriage should be quoted as a success or a failure was a moot point. She felt that during the first years of Meg's life it had at least been on the way to success. And then the estrangement had come, and she still didn't know the cause, though she still suspected it must have had something to do with the old rumours about herself and Tom. But they had never discussed the matter, never even admitted that there was a rift.

Ellen sighed.

No, she could hardly follow that line of argument. Love as a basis for marriage must be left out of their considerations. In the end she grounded her objections on the fact that Meg had seen too little of the world and led too retired a life to be in a position to make a sensible choice.

'Perhaps,' she suggested, 'perhaps she ought to go out and about a bit more. And perhaps it's time she stopped having lessons with Miss Hamilton. If she's to make the right decisions about her adult life she shouldn't be leading the life of a schoolgirl any longer. Besides, I think she's maybe outgrowing the need for regular instruction. Miss Hamilton told me the other day that she is working less well. Her mind doesn't seem to be on her work as before.'

'I'm not surprised,' remarked Donald. 'No room for deponent verbs in a head that's full of wedding finery. Are you suggesting we tell Miss Hamilton it's time to go?'

'I think that might be the best thing. After all, Meg will be seventeen next month. That seems quite a good opportunity to put an end to the arrangement. And we could perhaps take Meg out and about a bit – concerts, plays, dinner parties, even . . . I don't know,' she sighed, aware of the added burden of social life this would imply.

Donald considered the matter for a moment. He had not forgotten his ineffectual approaches to Miss Hamilton. He had been both humiliated by her rejection of him and filled with admiration for her steadfast sense of duty to Meg. The desire to try again, and succeed this time, had been with him ever since. But he was a man who knew how to wait. He had waited for years for Ellen, and he could wait a few years for this woman, knowing that the one insuperable barrier, her position in the household as Meg's governess, would inevitably be removed in the course of time. And now, ironically enough, it was Ellen herself who was suggesting a curtailment of his waiting. Life, he decided, sometimes had its unexpected little bonuses.

'If that's what you want,' he said, trying to sound indifferent, 'you can go ahead and tell Miss Hamilton.'

'Don't you think it should be you who tells her?'

But Donald was adamant. He felt his chances of success would be seriously diminished if Miss Hamilton suspected that her dismissal was in any way due to eagerness on his part for the present arrangement to come to an end. He was sure that one of the best cards he had to play was his scrupulous adherence to the decision that as long as Meg needed a governess he should not interfere. No, for once Ellen was going to have to tackle a problem without the help of her husband. It was, after all, he pointed out, her own idea. Ellen was not given to having ideas, not where practical matters were concerned, and decided that in future she would do better to revert to her usual state of passivity.

Meg was disconcerted when she heard that her lessons were soon to come to an end, but on the whole she was less upset about it than could have been expected, given her attachment to Miss Hamilton and the enjoyment she had always got out of her lessons – up till recently, that is. But during the past few months she had worked less willingly and less joyfully, absorbed as she was in projecting herself into married life and Kintalloch. The fact that she had not felt at liberty to mention to Miss Hamilton the very thing that was so much on her mind had also added to the mild estrangement that had come between her and her teacher.

Miss Hamilton guessed that Meg must be in love, but had been given no idea of who the young man of her choice might be. Knowing what an extremely retired life the girl led, it had occurred to her that it might be one of the two Kintalloch cousins. *Faute de mieux,* she added mentally. Then she reprimanded herself for her unfairness. After all, she didn't know the young men in question. No doubt they were perfectly amiable and admirable. But the fact remained that the poor girl never really saw anyone her own age.

All this was about to alter now. Meg was quite excited at the thought of the social panorama that lay before her.

In the event, she discovered that she hated this new social life. Perhaps because she was accompanied by a reluctant mother who could give to the social round as little pleasure as she received from it. Perhaps because the cloistered existence she had led so far had left her quite unfitted for the life to which she was now exposed. She knew none of the young people she was asked to mix with, knew none of their idols or catch-phrases, and she had no stock of frivolous subjects to discuss with them. She was afraid to open her mouth, knowing that nearly everything she might say would sound pedantic to them.

She missed Miss Hamilton more than she had expected.

Altogether, it was a miserable time for Meg – and for her mother too. But Ellen, at least, was sustained by the conviction that she was doing her duty by her daughter. If after a year or two Meg still wanted to marry Gavin, then so be it. She would at least have met some other young men. Meanwhile, privately, seeing the rather worldly young of her husband's colleagues, Ellen felt there was much to be said for an honest, steady young man like Gavin.

10

Miss Hamilton took her unexpected dismissal with dignity and understanding, although it came as an unwelcome surprise to her. She had assumed that the arrangement would go on till Meg was eighteen. For a moment she wondered whether this change of plan could have anything to do with the father's previous attentions to her. But that had been more than two years ago, and she was sure he must have forgotten all about her by now. Besides, both Meg and her mother had made it clear that it was Mrs Crombie's idea that Meg should leave the school room and step out into the adult world. She was a little hurt by the lightness with which Meg seemed to accept the end of their long relationship, but made allowances for the fact that the girl was almost certainly in love.

Miss Hamilton was also aware of the fact that the friendship between them had never been allowed to flourish as she would have liked. After the father had made his unexpected overtures she decided that she couldn't ask Meg back to her house, as that might have been taken as a desire on her part to see the same situation arise again. So her relationship with Meg had never got beyond the school room. All the same, she couldn't help feeling a little hurt by Meg's silence on the very subject that appeared to be occupying her mind almost to the exclusion of everything else. Even her favourite authors, both English and French, no longer aroused the usual fervent response.

The day after she had taken leave of Meg and her mother Miss Hamilton was sitting in her little parlour, feeling rather aimless, when she heard the garden gate being closed. Looking out of the window she saw Donald walking along the path towards the house. To her annoyance she felt a surge of excitement. This is not what I want at all, she told herself firmly, and had sufficiently controlled her feelings by the time she opened the door to greet him in her usual, composed manner.

'I've come to speak to you about Meg,' he said.

She ushered him into the sitting room and they both sat down. 'And how is Meg?'

'She was a bit tearful this morning, partly because she's just realized that she's going to miss you terribly, and partly because she feels she's behaved badly to you.'

'In what way?'

'Well, I only found out in the course of our conversation this morning that she had said nothing to you about the subject that has occupied her mind so entirely over the past few months. I presume you can guess what it is.'

'*Amor, amoris*?'

'Exactly. She considers herself unofficially engaged to her cousin Gavin, who is out in France fighting for us all. Her mother and I insisted that she was to tell no-one, as she's really too young to be engaged. It appears that she assumed that this no-one included you, and feels she has not been as frank with you as she would have liked.'

'Poor little Meg!'

'Yes, I know. But she has to grow up, and learning about the problems posed by conflicting loyalties is part of it. I wanted you to know because I realize how fond of her you are.'

'Thank you. I appreciate that. I am glad indeed that it was not indifference on her part that kept her silent. She is a quiet sort of person by nature but not, I think, secretive. It's nice to know that she was merely carrying out what she took to be her duty. And you think she will be happy with this young man?'

'*Qui sait?* He's a fine upstanding young fellow, and the family connexions are obviously unimpeachable.'

'But what sort of a companion will he be for Meg? Do they have much in common, beyond family connexions? Do they have the same tastes? Does he read? Does he think?'

'No more than is strictly necessary, I'm afraid. If Meg retains her love of language and literature he won't exactly be a soul mate to her. All I can say is that it promises to be no more disastrous than the average marriage. And it may never come off. If Meg gets the glimpse of the *beau monde* that her mother is plotting for her, she may change her mind and decide against Gavin.'

'I'm glad you came and told me all this. I feel a little less disoriented now. Dear Meg! I hope she enjoys her new life.'

'I know how fond of her you are. I know it to my cost, if you remember.'

Miss Hamilton had a struggle with herself. She realized where the conversation was going, and knew she ought to stop it. She said nothing. For once she decided to let events take their course, and not intervene, not even in the name of a morality she fully approved.

This time Donald found the eloquence that had evaded him before. He pointed out that there was no longer her duty to Meg keeping them apart, and that he had accepted her decision, and done nothing to interfere with that duty. He had waited patiently and in silence.

'But my heart has not been silent,' he continued. 'Every day I've heard it beating to the sound of your name – Matilda, Matilda, Matilda.'

They were silent for a moment.

Then he continued:

'You were asking about the intellectual affinity between Meg and Gavin. They have little in common, yet they will probably marry. You and I have so much that we could share, and yet . . . '

' . . . and yet the world does not allow us to be friends,' she concluded.

Two hours later they were sitting together on the couch, still talking. They had decided to disregard the world. Donald told her of the long-standing estrangement between himself and

Ellen. Matilda Hamilton had heard nothing of the rumours about the supposed incest. She felt she ought to urge him to forget about them and heal the breach – but it was too late now. She could not bear to think of abandoning this happiness that had come within her reach. This time, she told herself, she was not going to let it go. She had had her share of renunciation – when Donald had first approached her, and also many years earlier, in her youth. Some day she would tell Donald about it. But today she wanted to concentrate on her present happiness.

As soon as she had heard that her employment with the Crombies was soon to be terminated she had started making enquiries about another post, and had received several replies. After Donald left she went to her desk, picked up the letters, and threw them into the fire. *'Alea jacta est,'* she murmured, as she turned away from the blaze. Donald would provide. With characteristic honesty she told herself that she was now going to be a kept woman. If that is the precondition of happiness, she thought, I accept it.

Days later, as they sat together looking at the fire, she said:

'It's funny how history repeats itself.'

'What history? This? You and I, you mean?'

Matilda nodded. 'It's all so long ago. More than twenty years. But it's exactly the same situation. I suppose it's one to which governesses are prone. I was with a family in London, and the husband and I fell in love. For a while we held out, then began meeting in secret – brief, fear-laden meetings. In the end we decided to run away together. We planned it all very skilfully. He was supposed to be going to a meeting in Paris. I was going to spend a holiday with what remained of my family after the débâcle. We met in Norwich and had three wonderful days together.'

'Including three wonderful nights?' asked Donald.

'Of course. We were so happy, we just didn't care what sort of a scandal there would be when people found out. And then I spoilt it all.'

'*You* did? When you were so happy?'

'Yes. In a way *because* I was so happy. My Calvinist upbringing got the better of me and I decided he had to go back to his wife and family. There was still time for him to get back when he was expected. I convinced him that even if he didn't go back I couldn't possibly stay with him. So he left, in time to avoid a scandal.'

'And you? What did you do?'

'I went home and sent a telegram to my employers saying my mother was very ill and that I'd have to stay at home and look after her. I expect most people thought it a bit odd, but no-one ever suspected the truth. I gather he has lived "happily" with his wife ever since.'

'And you?' Donald asked again.

'I made a mess of things at home. I had to give some reason for the fact that I wasn't going back, and I didn't do it convincingly enough. Partly because of that, and partly because I felt I had to confess to someone, I told one of my sisters. She was horrified and told my mother, who immediately convened a family council. They agreed *en masse* that I was a scarlet woman, and threw me out. And that was it. I've been on my own ever since. Thank goodness I had the makings of a good teacher in me. That has been my salvation, financially and emotionally. But it's always sad, in the long run. You are given the loan of someone else's children for a few years, and then they grow up and you lose them. Oh, some of them keep in touch, but it's not the same. It's the daily propinquity that counts. When that goes, everything changes. And now Meg, the dearest and sweetest of them all . . . ' She sighed.

'This time,' he said, 'you've got me instead. I know you've lost Meg, but at least it was in the natural course of events, not because of accepting me.'

'I know,' she said, laying her head on his shoulder. 'One loses them all, sooner or later. This is the first time I've had any compensation. I can hardly complain, can I?'

78

They soon fell into a comfortable routine. Donald arrived in the evening two or three times a week, and stayed till late at night. The neighbours soon got to know, of course, and it wasn't long till they started looking the other way whenever they encountered Matilda in the street. She had known this would happen, but that didn't make it any less humiliating. What added to the unpleasantness was the fact that she felt sure the neighbours were in the right. Not only was she breaking the moral code, but she was also breaking one of the strictest of social laws. And she was not an iconoclast by nature. Everything has to be paid for, she would tell herself whenever these considerations tended to depress her. It's not a lot to pay for Donald's love. Then she smiled, as she thought of his answer when she had voiced her misgivings and pricks of conscience.

'*Vivamus mea Lesbia atque amemus,*' he had quoted.

Catullus again, she thought, and remembered Meg's indignation over the term *passer*. Sparrow indeed! It was a full-grown canary that had died. She now wondered whether the name 'Lesbia' was perhaps equally unsuitable. As far as she knew, the Lesbia in question had not been too amiable a character. Well, she thought, I'm sure there are plenty of people who would say the same of me. My neighbours, for instance. And she resolutely dismissed the subject from her mind without going any further into the list of people who might have reason to criticise her.

One evening just before Christmas, Donald appeared carrying a large and apparently heavy parcel.

'Donald, what is it?' she asked.

'Father Christmas!' he replied, setting the parcel carefully down on the table. As he took the wrapping off she saw a gramophone appear, and a box of records.

He cut short her protestations and thanks, and began winding the instrument. 'Go and sit down by the fire,' he said, 'I don't want you to know what I'm going to play first.'

'Oh, Donald! Do tell,' she pleaded.

'All right,' he said, still winding. 'It's the Emperor.'

'How lovely!' She sat still and composed herself to listen carefully. Donald finished the winding process, picked a needle out of a small tin box and carefully inserted it in the gramophone head. Then he opened the box with the records, took one out and placed it on the turntable.

'Now!' he exclaimed, and the music began.

As soon as she heard the first notes of the introduction Matilda burst out laughing.

'Oh, that Emperor! I thought you meant Beethoven.'

'I thought you might. You're the sort of woman who always thinks of Beethoven first. But this is for dancing. Up you get.'

'We can't dance here, in this tiny room,' she protested.

'Yes, we can.' Donald was moving about quickly, pushing the chairs and small articles of furniture out of the way. As the music came to the last of the introductory bars he bowed deeply in front of her.

'May I have the pleasure of this dance?'

She stood up and they danced, hesitatingly at first as the waltz theme appeared, then with growing confidence. Neither had danced for years, but soon they forgot this and gave themselves up to their enjoyment.

'I might have known you would be a good dancer,' he said. 'You do everything well. And this is my favourite waltz.'

'Now it's mine too,' she said. 'And if I dance well it's because I have such a good partner.'

'We're a wonderful couple, aren't we?'

Just then they swirled round a little too near the fireplace and Donald's foot caught on the hearthrug. They lost their balance and fell, laughing, on to the couch.

'Pride, you see,' he gasped, still laughing.

'The inevitable fall,' she agreed. And she was so happy that she didn't even think the word 'fall' with a capital F.

11

When the Great War ended and the young men started coming back from the front, Meg felt enormous relief. Partly because Gavin had come through the ordeal, and partly because it would shortly signify an end to the social round she so hated. She had never been able to form any real friendship with any of her companions. The boys she found utterly uninteresting and much too young, as all the older ones were in the forces. As for the girls, none seemed to share her interests. And besides, even when she made an effort to meet them on their own ground and talk about fashions and dances and film stars, she was hampered all the time by the fact that she was not to mention the one thing that was of most importance to her, her hope of soon being able to marry Gavin.

She felt insincere all the time.

How could she say freely what she thought about anything, when her feelings about everything were coloured by what she felt for Gavin?

She thought things would be better once she was able to talk about her engagement; but, as it turned out, the revelation did nothing for her in the circle of her friends and acquaintances. They all made it clear that they thought she had been very sly in concealing such an important fact from them.

'But my parents wouldn't let me tell anyone,' she protested. 'They said I was too young.'

None of them accepted this as an excuse. It was evident that her idea of filial obedience was ridiculously out of date, positively pre-war. One of them summed it all up scornfully with the words:

'She's nothing but a Little Victorian Miss.'

Ellen too had had enough of social life, and readily agreed that the wedding should not be put off any longer.

Meg felt her happiness should now be complete. That it wasn't she attributed to a number of different causes: all the bother and decisions which a wedding involved, uncertainty as to where they were to live, and fear of having to play the leading role in any ceremony, even in such a quiet wedding. Once it was all over, she knew for certain that she would be the happiest of mortals.

The problem of where the young couple was to live exercised the whole family for some time. Tom thought Meg and Gavin ought to move into one of the home farms, so that the young people could have a house to themselves, unencumbered by in-laws. Meg wasn't convinced she could cope with a place of her own, and Bessie was perfectly sure that she couldn't.

'She's Ellen's daughter,' she reminded her husband. 'You know what that means. She doesn't know a thing about running a house. Even with two servants she'd never manage.'

'Well, you managed. At the same age, you walked in and took over the whole place, not just one of the farmhouses.'

Bessie laughed. 'Ah, but I had a vocation. I wanted to be mistress of Kintalloch. After all, that was why I married you, wasn't it?'

Tom laughed too. 'Well, whatever your motives, you made a very good job of it from the first.'

'Besides,' continued Bessie, 'she's such a dreamy little thing. Even if she'd been taught, she would have a struggle.'

'She did have an excellent governess!'

'You know very well what I mean. Miss Hamilton taught her a lot of French and Latin, and how to write a sonnet, no doubt. But I don't think she told her anything about how to supervise the servants, or how to make marmalade, or how to order enough meat to keep a canary happy.'

'Are canaries carnivores?' asked Tom with mock seriousness.

'All right, all right. Is that what you would call a mixed metaphor?'

'Certainly it was pretty mixed. But I know what you mean.

Perhaps it would be a good idea for them to start off here, with Meg under your supervision. Then they could move out later on. Or perhaps we could.'

'*We?* Move out? Whatever for?'

'To give Gavin a chance. After all, I've had more than twenty-five years of running the show. I'm glad I was young when I took the whole thing over. It might be a good idea for Gavin to do the same. We could move out to Nether Kintalloch in a few years and enjoy a life of ease. How does that strike you?'

'Hmm!' was the reply. 'I don't think it's time to be thinking along those lines yet. Perhaps when I'm old and grey.'

'And full of sleep . . . '

Bessie gave him a puzzled look.

'Look, Mother, this looks like Miss Hamilton's writing.'

Meg handed the envelope to her mother. She was eager to know whether Miss Hamilton had accepted the invitation to the wedding. She still missed her governess, and wished their separation had not been so total. Perhaps if I'd had a little more initiative, she thought, I might have done something about it. An invitation to the wedding had seemed a good idea, as a means of closing the gap.

'Oh!' Ellen sounded quite disconcerted. 'She says she can't come. She has a previous engagement. But there's a letter for you here. Perhaps she'll be more explicit.'

Meg took the letter eagerly, and read:

Dear Meg,

I am truly sorry that I shall not be able to come to your wedding, which is to take place in the middle of a long overdue visit to my family. You cannot imagine how sorry I am that I shall not be there with you on such a happy occasion. Our paths ran parallel for some years, and they were the happiest of my teaching career. Now they have diverged, and must inevitably move further apart in the course of the years. I shall always think with affection of our many hours together.

    With heartfelt wishes for your future happiness,

    I remain,

    Your most sincere well-wisher,

    Matilda Hamilton.

Meg handed the letter over to her mother in silence. She was distressed by its obviously valedictory tone.

After reading it Ellen said:

'Well, it's certainly affectionate enough. I wondered whether she felt any resentment over the fact that your classes stopped earlier than was expected. But that's evidently not the case. I think I should keep that letter, if I were you, Meg. It's quite a testimonial.'

'Should I reply, do you think?'

'No, I don't think that's called for. After all, her letter is a reply to our invitation. If we always had to reply to replies we'd never be done, would we?'

Meg agreed. But once again she felt a sense of regret at the thought that Miss Hamilton didn't seem to have a place in her life any longer.

Matilda had written the letter with a heavy heart. She and Donald had agreed that she couldn't possibly go to the wedding, and he had done his best to make sure that she didn't get an invitation, stressing the fact that it was to be such a quiet wedding, almost a family affair.

But Meg had insisted, and he felt he dare not intervene. It would have been enough for Matilda to know that Meg wanted her to be there. When he lost the argument and the invitation was sent out they decided that all she could do was allege a previous engagement, and accompany the formal reply with a more personal letter to Meg herself. But the incident saddened Matilda, and for some time after, nasty little feelings of guilt kept edging their way into her mind.

* * *

After a short honeymoon Meg and Gavin moved in with his parents. Bessie immediately set to work on Meg, determined to turn her into an able housekeeper, and Gavin accompanied his father on the daily round on the estate. Tom had followed in his father's footsteps, and had taken care from the start that his sons, especially the elder, knew all about looking after the land and its dependents. During the last years of the war he had had to see to everything himself, while the boys were away in France, and now he was glad of some help, even though Gavin was the only one who had come back.

Angus had developed a taste for things French during his war service and was now in Paris, pursuing some course in literary studies. Meg thought this sounded absolutely thrilling, remembering her lessons with Miss Hamilton. To think that he'd be able to go to the Comédie Française, and see Molière and Racine – properly acted, and all in French! None of the rest of the household shared her enthusiasm. While agreeing that it was up to him to choose his own life, they all felt it was a pity he had not decided to come back home.

Talking about it with Gavin one evening Meg remarked:

'He was never quite as devoted to Kintalloch as you are, was he?'

'Not really. As he himself put it, perhaps it had something to do with his being a younger son.'

Meg stared at him in surprise. 'Why should that make him less devoted to the place? Oh, I see,' she added, 'because he'll never inherit, you mean?'

'Something of the sort. I think nature got us the wrong way round. He's an impatient, passionate sort of character. I don't think he terribly likes doing as he's told. Whereas I'm a quiet, accommodating sort of a chap. I don't think I'd have minded toeing the line quite so much. But then, of course, I've always known that sooner or later I'd be in sole charge.'

Meg smiled. 'Anyway, I think you're right. You're a *much* more accommodating person than Angus is. That's why you'll make such a splendid job of running the estate. I can see they all love you.'

'So Mother Nature got it right after all?' queried Gavin.

Meg was putting a great deal of effort into learning how to run an establishment. She enjoyed her long sessions with Aunt Bessie, who could always be counted on to see the funny side of something, even Meg's worst mistakes. Even if she broke a favourite cup, or ordered three times as much milk as they needed, Aunt Bessie could always turn the event into a joke, so that Meg didn't feel too bad about it. But she did find it all very tiring. She wasn't used to any kind of responsibility, and, above all, she simply wasn't used to *doing* things – not anything that required physical movement, that is. She had spent most of her life sitting at a desk or in an armchair. The almost permanent sensation of tiredness, along with her natural tendency to undervalue her own capabilities, meant that she made slow progress in spite of her good intentions.

Bessie, who all her life had been strong as an ox, failed to see what a strain she was putting on her new daughter-in-law. She realized that Meg was riddled with self-doubt, and did all she could to encourage her. She would have liked to see the girl take a more enterprising line – at least, she thought that was what she would have liked. But Bessie was by nature a leader and organiser, and was happy to take over whenever Meg fell by the wayside.

One of the things that tired Meg, quite apart from the physical effort involved in being on the go so much of the time, was the constant company and non-stop conversation. She was used to spending hours by herself, or in the company of her mother, another devotee of silence. There was no such thing as an awkward silence between Meg and her mother. Silence was the normal mode of their existence, into which they dropped the odd morsel of conversation now and then. This was something Meg had never thought of before. All her visits to Kintalloch had been just that: visits; holidays in which a completely different set of rules applied. It was all stimulating and absorbing and delightful. And then she went back to the peace and silence of the Edinburgh house and recovered her balance. Now there seemed to be no space or time for recovery, and she struggled on, always hoping that soon, soon, she would be able to cope with it all.

One day Bessie had been called away and Meg sat down for a minute's rest in the sitting room. Tom came in and found her there, lying back with her eyes closed.

'Tired, Meg?' he asked.

She sat up suddenly. 'Oh, it's you, Uncle Tom. I didn't hear you coming in.'

Tom sat down opposite her.

'You haven't answered me. Are you tired?'

'Just a little.' Meg looked across at him and suddenly realized that he too looked weary as he sat almost slumped in his chair.

'You're tired too, aren't you?'

'Just a little. Like you. It's a tiring business.'

'What is?'

'Life.'

Meg smiled. 'It seems to be. Well, just some of the time,' she added.

That night she mentioned the incident to Gavin.

'Yes, I've noticed it too. He often looks tired. I must try to take as much off his shoulders as I can. After all, that's what he did. He gave up his university studies to come home and look after things for his father.'

'Yes, but his father was ill. He was already a very sick man, wasn't he? You don't think . . . you don't think your father's ill, do you?' Meg asked anxiously.

'Probably not. But he is over fifty now. I know it's not a great age, but some people just seem to wear out sooner than others.'

Meg looked at him and thought how like his father he was, as she remembered him from her childhood – tall and strong and indestructible-looking.

'I hope you don't take after him in that respect,' she said.

He laughed. 'Never fear. I take after my mother – a steam-roller could run over her and she'd come up smiling.'

They had been married for two years before Meg became pregnant. All the family was delighted with the news. Meg's joy was tempered by a feeling of awe. She felt it was an immense responsibility to have another life inside her, and she read up as much as she could about how to conduct her pregnancy.

All the others wanted to wrap her in cotton wool. Bessie was sure she should be giving up all her household duties in order to rest more.

'Is that what you did?' Meg sounded amused and sceptical.

'No, but I'm as strong as a horse, not a delicate little creature like you.'

Meg, however, maintained that normal life was recommended by her books, and for once found the strength to stick up for her own ideas, and kept to her usual routine in the house. After three months she lost the child. Bessie was disconsolate, and blamed herself for not insisting on more rest. A year later Meg became pregnant again, and agreed to obey orders and take things easy. Again she lost the child at three months. Nobody knew quite whom or what to blame this time.

It was two years before the next pregnancy. This time the three-month danger period passed by without any problems, and she began to feel more confident. All went well till the actual birth. Then everything went wrong. The child was stillborn, and Meg nearly lost her life. It was some time before they had the courage to tell her that she would never be able to have a child.

For months Meg led a twilight life, hardly aware of anything except her misery. In addition to her grief over the child, the knowledge that she could never give Gavin the heir he so wanted was almost more than she could bear. She felt she had failed them all, not only Gavin and his parents, but also her own mother – who, rather to her surprise, had shown a great interest in the prospect of becoming a grandmother.

The thought of having a grandchild had indeed moved Ellen strangely. Looking back over her life, she felt she had never been happy from the age of seven till the arrival of her daughter had brought hope and love and comfort to her life. It had been during the first five years of Meg's life that she and Donald had come nearest to a genuine understanding of each other. All that had disappeared, since his sudden estrangement from her; but the thought of this new life coming into the family filled her with hope and comfort.

The knowledge that this child would be equally descended from Tom and from her was also a source of hope. Perhaps their grandchild would do something to bring Tom and her a little closer again. She had suffered great losses in her life – night-time separation from Tom imposed by their parents, the loss of a sense of innocence in her love for him, the misery caused by all the rumours about them, the estrangement from Donald – but worse than any of these had been the growing indifference she had felt in Tom ever since his marriage.

And now she had lost the hope of a grandchild to bring them together again. Once more she became convinced of the ineradicable hostility of the world.

12

'There's your tea,' said Matilda, handing Donald his cup. 'Oh, I've forgotten the biscuits.'

'I'll get them,' he volunteered, reaching to put his cup down.

But Matilda was already up.

'It's all right,' she said, 'I'd better go myself. I bought some more today, and I can't quite remember where I left them.'

She went into the kitchen and picked up the empty biscuit barrel from its place, then found the new supply of biscuits and filled the barrel. As she turned to go back she heard a strange little cry coming from the sitting room, and then Donald's voice groaning:

'Oh, no! Oh, no!'

She ran back and reached his side just in time to catch the cup of hot tea before it slid off the saucer in his shaking hand. He was sitting in the armchair, slumped over to one side. She knelt beside him and looked into his face. His eyes were staring straight ahead, evidently not focusing. His mouth was twisted to one side, and half open. A thin stream of tea was trickling down his chin.

'Donald! Donald!' she called urgently, but could evoke no response. She left him and ran out of the house, knowing she must get help, with a vague idea of going to one of the neighbours and asking them to send for a doctor. In spite of their continued ostracism, she was sure they couldn't refuse. But before she got to the garden gate she saw a policeman solemnly walking his beat, a little further along the street. She ran to enlist his help.

'We'll have an ambulance along in no time at all, ma'am,' he assured her.

She ran back to the house.

Donald was in the same position, and still seemed unaware of what was going on.

Matilda was overcome by a sense of helplessness, and railed at her own ignorance. Why had she never found out what to do in such a case? She was sure he had had a stroke, but what should she be doing about it while she waited for the ambulance? He looked most uncomfortable, all fallen over to the side of his chair like that. Should she get him on to the floor? She was afraid to try. For one thing, it might be the worst thing to do. She just didn't know. Besides, Donald had put on weight in the past few years. He was now a heavy man. If she tried moving him she might only let him fall, and perhaps even break a bone. She knelt beside him, holding his hands, calling his name, and getting no response. After what seemed an eternity the ambulance arrived. She followed the stretcher out of the house.

'I'm coming too,' she said.

The men raised no objection, but pointed out she'd better get her coat and hat. It was a cold evening, and she'd have quite a long walk back from the hospital.

In the Infirmary she sat in a draughty corridor for what seemed another eternity, waiting for news. Ellen would have to be told, of course. But Matilda felt she could do nothing till someone told her about Donald's condition. She couldn't even decide how to contact Ellen, how to break the news to her. All she could do was wait and grieve.

At last a tall, thin, bored-looking doctor came.

'Well, Mrs Crombie,' he began.

'I'm not Mrs Crombie,' she interrupted. Life was going to be complicated enough without any misunderstandings about her identity.

The doctor looked at her in silence.

'I'm just a friend,' she added.

'But there is a Mrs Crombie?'

'Yes.'

'I . . . ah . . . see. Well, Miss . . . ah?'

'Hamilton,' she said, exasperated at the delay. 'What's the situation with Mr Crombie? Is he very ill?'

'Well, Miss . . . ah . . . Hamilton, it's a bit soon to give an exact diagnosis yet. It may, it just might, be an ischemic episode.'

'And that is?'

'It's something very like a stroke, with the difference that, in such a case, the damage is not irreversible. But, as I said, it's too soon to tell.'

Matilda was left with the faint hope that things might not be quite as bad as they looked. The doctor handed her over to one of the nurses, who took all the particulars and said that, all things considered, she thought it would be better if Mrs Crombie heard the news of her husband's illness through the hospital. This was a relief to Matilda, till she realized that now all she had to do was go home and wait for the morning. Then she would have to come and enquire as to Donald's condition. No-one would go to any trouble to keep her informed. As far as the hospital was concerned, the only person who had to be informed was the wife.

13

Life had been rather pleasanter for Ellen lately.

She had become reconciled to the fact that she was never going to have the longed-for grandchild, and Meg seemed, at long last, to be beginning to recover her strength, if not her spirits. But that, surely, would follow. Life at home was quiet and peaceful, the way she liked it. Donald was out at work all day, and frequently out in the evening, with friends or at some meeting or other. It had become such an established thing that she no longer even bothered to ask where he was going. She knew he was still very friendly with Martin Carr, and assumed he spent much of his time with him. Martin, who had been told of Donald's involvement with Matilda, had been primed, and was always ready to corroborate if necessary.

After years of doubts and hesitations, Ellen had started writing poetry. At first the intention was never to show it to anyone. But as her confidence grew with practice, she began to think that some day – perhaps in the distant future – she might even try to publish some of the less personal poems.

Looking over her productions she came to the conclusion that they were all exceedingly introspective. Even those that made no reference to her personal circumstances, and which she might therefore contemplate showing to someone else, were so concerned with her own private form of speculation that she wondered whether they would be of any general interest.

Well, she thought, time would tell.

Ellen herself was in no hurry. It amused her to think that a woman who hadn't even started writing till well into her fifties should have this leisurely attitude to her work. As if I thought I was going to live for ever, she mused, with a wry smile. But whether she tried to publish or not, the important thing was to keep on writing. She had done so little in her life – brought up one daughter, that was all, and even that had been with the tireless help of the devoted Miss Hamilton. It was a source of great satisfaction to her to feel she was accomplishing something at last, on her own. She also felt she was gaining some insight into her own turbulent, unavowable emotions, simply by trying to write about them. If, into the bargain, she had managed to produce a few poems that were worth reading in their own right, so much the better.

Yes, she had no doubt at all, she must go on writing. At the beginning she had stuck to the conventional forms, welcoming the framework that rhyme and a fixed metre gave. But lately she had ventured into *vers libre*, not without misgivings, feeling lost and vulnerable in these uncharted seas.

She was sitting in her bedroom one evening, where she did all her writing, when she heard the telephone ringing. She got up, went out into the hall, and picked up the receiver. A strange voice at the other end was asking to speak to Mrs Crombie.

When Ellen got to the Infirmary, Donald was lying just as Matilda had seen him, slightly twisted to one side, with his mouth askew and his eyes staring. He appeared to be unconscious.

When she spoke to him the nurse said:

'It's no use, Mrs Crombie. He can't hear you. Even if he could, he can't reply.'

This nurse had just come on duty and couldn't tell her anything about what had happened. Ellen had to go to the office for the information. There she was told by a disconcertingly sympathetic young woman that he appeared to have had a stroke. So far the prognosis was doubtful. It was just a case of waiting.

When Ellen asked about how he had got there the girl became even more sympathetic.

'Sit down, Mrs Crombie,' she said. 'I'll tell you all I know, which isn't much. He was brought in a while ago on a stretcher by one of our ambulance crews. He was at a friend's house when he had the stroke.'

Ellen's thoughts immediately flew to Martin Carr. But she couldn't understand why Martin hadn't contacted her himself.

'Did he say who he was?' she asked.

'Who?' asked the girl. At that moment it seemed an utterly stupid question to Ellen. Later she realized that the girl had understood her misapprehension and was playing for time.

'The friend, of course,' she replied sharply.

'Well, actually, the fact is . . . it was a lady.'

Ellen smothered a gasp. 'And did she say who she was?'

The girl nodded. 'Yes, she said she was a Miss Hamilton.'

Ellen gripped her handbag fiercely and told herself that it was, after all, a very common name in Scotland. In Edinburgh alone there must be dozens of Miss Hamiltons. Then, trying to control the tremor in her voice, she asked:

'Did she give her address?'

The girl consulted the report in front of her.

'Twenty-two Waverton Gardens,' she read out. 'Shall I write it down for you?'

'No. Thank you. I shan't forget.'

Ellen went back to the ward and sat down beside Donald. He hadn't moved. She sat beside him through the night, almost as motionless as he was, disregarding the nurses who urged her to go home.

In the morning they managed to persuade her to leave. The ward had to be free of visitors to let the cleaners take over, and then the doctors had to do their rounds. And besides, there would be no news till he had been examined again by his doctor.

She went home and tried to decide what to do. She kept telling herself that Donald might have been there for some perfectly innocent reason. She tried to think of one, and couldn't. He's been carrying on an affair with her, she told herself – there's no other explanation. I wonder how long this has been going on. Suddenly it struck her that this might explain Donald's estrangement all those years ago. But no. Meg was only five at the time, and they hadn't engaged Miss Hamilton till five years later. So it couldn't be that.

But then, perhaps they had known each other already when the appointment was made. Perhaps her coming to them as governess was an arranged thing. The thought that this woman might have been frequenting their house all those years while having an affair with her husband filled Ellen with revulsion. And to think that at the same time that woman was in charge of the education of their child! In the midst of her shock Ellen was able to register a feeling of incredulity on this point. She just couldn't believe that the Miss Hamilton she had known could be capable of such treachery. The odd thing was that she had less difficulty in imagining her husband capable of it. And yet all her anger was directed at the mistress, not at the husband. Was this perhaps because of the pitiable state she saw him in?

Then she thought of Martin Carr, and decided to consult him. He came round as soon as he got her message. He confessed that he had been aware of the liaison from the start, and had known that Donald often claimed to be with him when he was in fact with Miss Hamilton.

'It was not a situation I enjoyed,' he admitted. 'It made me feel very disloyal to you.'

'But your first loyalty was to Donald?'

'No, it wasn't even that. I knew I couldn't stop him from seeing her, whatever I did. So the only thing I could do, it seemed to me, was to help keep you from knowing what was going on. We had both hoped you would never find out.' He then went on to tell her how Miss Hamilton had refused to have anything to do with Donald while she was teaching Meg, and that she had chosen to go on teaching her rather than accept Donald as a lover and abandon Meg.

'Are you trying to defend this . . . this viper to me?' flashed Ellen.

'No, I can't defend her. But later on perhaps you'll be able to see . . . '

'Her point of view? Is that what you mean?'

'Not even that. That may be too much to expect. All I mean is that things could have been even worse.'

'Quite a recommendation!' she remarked bitingly.

After a while she recovered some of her habitual control and was able to spare a thought for Martin's feelings.

'This must be a great shock to you too – the illness, I mean. After all, you've been friends since you were children, haven't you?'

'Yes,' he said, 'it's a shock and perhaps a warning.'

'A warning?'

'To a contemporary. It could happen to any of us. And I'm sure Donald would have given a great deal for it not to have happened in this way, causing such distress all round.'

'By "all round" you mean to his family, his friends and . . . to her?'

'Yes. I don't think any of us are in an enviable position.'

At this point they were still trying to believe that Donald would recover, and that the worst aspect of the situation was the awkwardness caused by the poor timing of his illness. A few hours earlier or later, and the scandal would have been avoided.

They went back to the hospital together to hear what the doctor had to say. As they were going along one of the long narrow passages they met a tall figure coming towards them. It was Matilda, and she stopped as soon as she recognized Ellen. Martin, who had never met Matilda, thought the woman had just stopped to let them pass. Ellen had stopped too, and he took her arm and guided her past the tall figure.

When they got to the end of the corridor Ellen turned to Martin. 'Have you ever met Miss Hamilton?' she asked.

'No, I've never set eyes on her.'

'Well, you have now.'

'That woman we've just passed?'

'That woman. I'm so thankful you were with me. I don't know

97

what I'd have done if I'd been alone. I don't know what I'd have said if she'd spoken to me.'

Martin was nodding thoughtfully. 'As I said before, things could be even worse than they are. That was an example. Goodness knows, though, they're bad enough as it is.'

In the ward they were told that there had been no change. It was looking increasingly unlikely that there would be any improvement. Donald might go on in his present state for a long time. On the other hand, he might die at any minute.

In the event it took him four years to die. Four years in which Matilda spent an hour at his side every morning; four years in which Ellen sat beside him all afternoon.

It was thanks to Martin that this tolerable arrangement was arrived at. He suggested to Ellen that she should tell the ward sister it was her intention to spend every afternoon with her husband and ask her to ensure that any other visitors should be given this information. At first Ellen was reluctant to enter into this arrangement, on the grounds that it made things too easy for her rival. But soon she realized that leaving it to chance, while making the situation more difficult for Matilda, would make it equally difficult for her. The one thing she wanted to avoid was another encounter. Martin also pointed out that they had no way of knowing whether Donald was aware of their presence. He realized it was hard for Ellen to accept that there were strong ties between her husband and this woman. To deprive him of her company, if indeed he was in any way aware of it, would surely be vindictive, in the face of the terrible situation Donald found himself in.

This idea provoked a fierce inner struggle in Ellen. She had seen herself as a powerless victim all her life. It was tempting to be able to punish the guilty, just as she, the innocent victim, had been punished throughout. While she hesitated, Martin said something about magnanimity.

Yes, she thought, that is my one hope. To feel at least that this has not lowered me in my own eyes.

'Very well,' she had said, 'that will be the best arrangement. Thank you. I'll tell the sister.'

So she spent every afternoon for four years sitting in silence beside her speechless and motionless husband. Sometimes she wondered whether she was achieving anything by the exercise, beyond her own peace of mind. But always the possibility that Donald might in some obscure way be aware of her presence, that his burden might be lightened by it, kept her from making any change in the routine. She knew that Matilda came every morning, and sometimes marvelled that the faithless Donald should be the recipient of such devotion from the two women in his life.

In her more bitter moments Ellen even suspected that both she and Matilda were perhaps motivated not so much by concern for him as by a desire to vie with each other in devotion and self-sacrifice.

Soon after Donald had been taken into hospital Matilda heard the doorbell ring one afternoon and opened the door to find Martin Carr on the doorstep. She recognized him as the man she had seen with Ellen, and guessed who it must be.

He had come, he explained, to clarify a rather delicate matter that must be giving her some concern.

'As you no doubt know, Donald and I have been close friends since we were at school together. He has kept me informed of all his business affairs. I understand that he has been contributing to your expenses for the last few years. Did he tell you about any long-term arrangements in this respect?'

'No. We never spoke about the future. In our irregular situation we felt it best just to live from day to day. I got the impression he was the sort of man who takes life as it comes.'

'Yes, in general that was the case.' Martin wondered whether she had noticed that they were speaking of Donald in the past tense. 'But in this case he showed more foresight. He told me some years ago that he had made an arrangement for an annuity to be paid to you for the rest of your life, regardless of whether he predeceased you or not. The documents are in my hands. He even made provision for the annuity to be paid in the event of his becoming incapable of administering his own affairs.'

'How extraordinary! As if he'd had a premonition.'

'I don't know about that. It's the sort of contingency a lawyer guards against automatically. I've no reason to believe he was given to premonitions, or anything like that.'

'No, I think you're probably right. Just the normal thing to do for a man in his position, with his training.'

'At any rate, I wanted you to know that your financial situation remains unchanged. Perhaps you've been too concerned about Donald to think of that just yet. But at least you can feel secure as far as that aspect of the matter is concerned.'

Matilda was touched, both by the knowledge of Donald's foresight and by Martin's consideration in coming to tell her. After she had expressed her gratitude they spoke of Donald's condition and his prospects.

'I'm afraid things could hardly be worse,' said Martin.

'They couldn't possibly be worse,' Matilda put in with energy. 'Death would be a thousand times preferable.'

'Yes, I suppose so,' said Martin thoughtfully. 'And yet – and yet . . . '

'But what possible advantage can there be in living such a life?' she cried.

'I don't know. But *dum spiro spero*. I don't mean in the ordinary sense. I know there's no hope of a recovery, or even a partial recovery. But, while there's life . . . '

'You mean life at any price? I think Donald would be the last person to want to live on such terms.'

'I agree. But still, we don't know whether there is any sort of consciousness there. If there isn't, then it doesn't matter, as far as he is concerned, whether he's alive or dead. But if there is, then . . . I'm a great optimist, Miss Hamilton. I feel we can all learn something from experience, however distressing it may be. Perhaps there is still something in Donald that is . . . advancing – would that be the word?'

Up till that point Matilda had spent her morning hours with Donald sitting beside him in speechless misery, feeling totally cut off from him. After that conversation with Martin she began to take a more active role. She now spent her hour with him holding his hand, stroking his poor, twisted face and talking, talking all the time. She spoke of their love for each other; of the happy times they had had together; of Meg.

Every so often one of the nurses would come and say:

'It's no use, Miss Hamilton. He can't hear you. You won't get an answer from him.'

And she would answer:

'I know, I know. But just in case . . . ' and the nurse would go away shaking her head. Matilda felt immensely grateful to Martin for suggesting that Donald might be, in some way hidden to them, advancing. Then it occurred to her that, in her life too, there was room for advancement. In her feelings about Ellen, for instance. In spite of being, as she herself admitted, the guilty party, she couldn't repress a feeling of hostility whenever she thought of the injured wife. Donald had assured her – with reason, she had felt – that Ellen did not love him and never had. But the knowledge that this allegedly indifferent wife spent every afternoon sitting beside her paralysed husband didn't seem to fit in with that statement. Some women, she knew, would do it to make a show of their devotion – the faithful wife forgiving her faithless husband. But from her many years in the household she knew Ellen well enough to realize that this reaction would have been totally out of character. Ellen was the last person to make a gesture, or play a part. So perhaps Donald had got it wrong, perhaps Ellen did love her husband. In that case she, Matilda, had done her incalculable harm. And the worst of it was that there was no way in which she could possibly make amends.

When she thought of Meg her feelings were equally unhappy. However carefully her mother might try to shield her, sooner or later she would be bound to discover the real circumstances attending her father's illness. What then would she think of the governess in whose charge she had spent so many years?

Meg, as it happened, had not found out about Miss Hamilton's involvement. She knew there had been a scandal, that her father had been taken ill in some other woman's house. But who that woman was Ellen managed to keep secret from her. Tom and Bessie knew, Gavin knew, but they were all only too eager to keep the truth from Meg, especially in her fragile state after losing all hope of a child. And the family had so few connexions outside their own intimate circle, even in Edinburgh, that they were able to keep the truth from her. Since her marriage Meg had hardly ever been in the city, and had lost touch with the few half-friends she had made during the year preceding her marriage.

Now she started coming through fairly regularly, just to be with her mother, who could no longer come and see her in Kintalloch, because of her daily vigil in the hospital. At first Meg went with Ellen, but she was so overcome at the sight of her father in his pitiable state that all she could do was sit by the bed while great tears rolled down her cheeks. After a few such visits Ellen decided it was too much of a strain on the girl, and refused to let her come. From then on Meg spent the afternoons in her own bedroom – where, as a girl, she used to sit at the window and read. Now she just sat and looked out at the gardens in front, and wondered whether life would ever again be worth living.

During her long hours at Donald's bedside Ellen often thought of the promise she had made herself before she married, that she would never love her husband. If she had kept that promise, what was she doing, sitting here at his bedside day after day? Was this simply the fulfilment of that other promise, that she would do everything in her power to be a good wife to Donald?

Did being a good wife necessarily imply being prepared to spend hours of every day sitting beside a living corpse?

Was this not going well beyond the minimum requirement?

And why was she doing it?

The only answer she could come up with was the thought that perhaps her presence could help Donald in some way. There might be something left in him that could respond to the vibrations of a friendly presence. Even if it were no more than that, it was worth doing for anyone in so bereft a state as Donald. Surely a few hours every day were not too much to give in such a cause?

At this point in her meditations it struck her that throughout her life she had given remarkably little time and attention to other people. Her immediate family, that was all. Even there she had handed over her child's education to a professional, not through lack of interest, but rather out of fear of not being up to the task.

She now realized that she knew nobody who had had anything like the amount of free time she had disposed of all her life. And what had she done with that time? Spent most of it brooding over the past or worrying about the future. For a while Ellen sat in total dejection. It seemed to her that she had never achieved anything. She had let her whole life be dominated by the scandal of her supposed incest with Tom. There had been no incest, but she had allowed the rumours to rule her life. She had taken on the role of innocent victim, and had assumed that this exonerated her from all efforts to lead a normal, active life.

What was worse, since examining the situation in her agonised poems, she realized that she was playing the part of innocent victim under false pretences. If Tom hadn't grown away from her, if Tom hadn't married Bessie . . . If Tom had given the slightest indication that he wanted to be her lover, she now realized, she would have accepted him.

That day she went home feeling chastened. She had seen into her heart as never before. It seemed to her that she had a lot to forgive herself, and that others had much to forgive her too.

Tout comprendre, c'est tout pardonner, she told herself.

At least she was beginning to understand. Perhaps the forgiveness would follow.

14

Donald had been sitting back in his chair and looking at the clock on the mantelpiece. Eight twenty-five. Eight twenty-five and all's well, he thought. He looked at the fire and felt its warmth all down his right side. He took a sip of the hot tea. Delicious. His usual sense of well-being at this stage of the evening seemed curiously heightened tonight. Warm fire, he thought, hot tea, and Matilda in the kitchen looking for the biscuits.

All's right with the world.

The words seemed to be the perfect expression of his present sense of plenitude. He took another sip of tea and turned to put the cup and saucer down on the little table Matilda had placed beside his armchair.

Or rather, he initiated the movement of turning to the left. But something seemed to be hindering him. It was as if, instead of turning to the left, he was being pushed, or perhaps pulled, to the right. He put more effort into the attempted movement, and suddenly felt overwhelmed. It wasn't pain, or nausea, or dizziness; just a sense of being overwhelmed by something immensely stronger than himself. He heard a little cry and the words *Oh, no! Oh, no!* but he didn't know that they had come from him. All he knew was this immense power, inside him and outside, forcing him to the right, while he struggled to keep the teacup steady. Nothing else mattered in the whole world. He was fighting a battle to hold the saucer firmly, so that the cup would not slide off it. All his energy and attention were concentrated on this. Then the cup disappeared, and he felt as if an immense black blind had been drawn before his eyes as he sank into unconsciousness.

There was nothing. No time, no place. No heat, no cold, no pain. Nothing. Not even the awareness of nothing. And, with time abolished, there was no way of knowing how long it took for the first faint shadow of awareness to come back. Hours? Days? Years?

Time was abolished. Place was abolished. There was neither sound nor sight. No memory, no sense of identity. Only, gradually and intermittently, a vague, faint shadow of awareness. A sort of pinkish glow took over. It was like being wrapped up in a warm, rosy cloud. Less tangible than a cloud. Just pink. Sometimes it was accompanied by a faraway sound, a series of gentle, irregular, soothing noises. Sometimes the pinkness came in silence. But always, awareness, when it came, was this soft, tender pink.

15

Life was quiet at Kintalloch.

Quiet and rather depressing. Donald's illness had come too soon after Meg had begun to recover from the loss of the baby and, with it, the hope of ever having a child. Gavin was concerned about her, so was Tom. Bessie too, but she was even more worried about the state of Tom's health. Although Gavin had taken over more and more of the responsibility for the estate, Bessie could see that Tom was finding it an effort to keep going. After some nagging from all three of them Tom promised to visit the doctor.

It was less easy to make Meg see reason. They were convinced that her frequent visits to Edinburgh were tiring her out, physically and emotionally. Although she soon gave up going to see her father, realizing that her uncontrollable weeping was doing nothing for him and putting an extra strain on her mother, she insisted on spending some time every week in town, so her mother could have her company in the mornings and evenings.

Tom went, as promised, to see his father-in-law, Dr Murdo, affectionately known to all and sundry as 'Doc'.

'Well, Tom,' said Doc as his son-in-law entered the room, 'have you come to tell me it's time I retired – still practising at my age, eh?'

'Far from it. I hope you're not contemplating anything of the sort. We all need you too much. I think it's more likely you'll tell me it's I who should be retiring.'

Doc gave a comfortable chuckle. 'Swinging the lead, I expect that's what it is. Playing the old soldier, eh? Well, I suppose we'd better examine you, or you'll say I'm not doing my job properly. Can't have you going to Bessie with complaints about me, can we?'

After he'd finished, Doc sat back in his chair and pushed his glasses up on to his forehead. Then he stretched his legs, folded his hands over his *embonpoint* and said:

'Seems to be the old ticker. Not doing as well as it should. But nothing to worry about, as long as you take things easy.'

'How easy?'

'More or less what you suggested. Retiring, or whatever it is a landowner does when he stops chasing all over his estate to see if there's a broken fence or a lost lamb requiring someone's attention. Just leave all that to Gavin. He's perfectly capable. Time you sat back and enjoyed a bit of a rest. And don't you argue about it. I know what I'm talking about.'

'I'm not thinking of arguing. Your word is law.'

Tom went away feeling ten years younger. For a long time he had been convinced that he had the same trouble as his father, so the diagnosis was no shock to him. The relief he felt stemmed from the fact that he had now been given permission to do what his body had been clamouring for, while his self-image had prevented him from sitting back and taking it easy. Now that it was official that this was what he must do, he could proceed with no loss of face. Besides, his retiring from the active scene would open the way to another project he had in mind.

They had a family council that evening. It was unanimously agreed that Tom was to stop going the rounds of the property. Gavin could manage that on his own. Tom would keep on doing some of the paper work, but no more than he could comfortably manage in a couple of hours. For the rest of the time he was to be free – to sit about watching other people working, or catching up on his reading in the library. Meg wondered whether anyone would suggest that Tom and Bessie should move out of the house and take up their abode in one of the home farms. This seemed to her the best possible arrangement, but she knew the suggestion couldn't come from her.

It came, in fact, from the most unexpected source, Bessie herself. And to everyone's surprise, it was Tom who objected.

'But I thought that was what you wanted,' exclaimed Bessie. 'You suggested it yourself long ago.'

'Yes, but things have changed. There's really too much work for Gavin to manage alone – don't interrupt, Gavin, I know what I'm talking about – and it seems to me that the best thing would be to get Angus to come home, if we can possibly tempt him away from Paris.'

'But why does that mean you have to stay in this house?' asked Gavin.

'You know what your brother's like. He can be quite a handful. We'll need your mother here to handle him. That not so, Bessie?'

Meg was a little disappointed. She felt it was now time for her to try running the house. With Aunt Bessie around she knew she would never get past the stage of apprentice. But she didn't have enough confidence to feel sure she would make a success of it, so her disappointment was tempered with some relief. It was also tempered with pleasurable expectation, for she and Angus got on well, and she had enjoyed his infrequent visits over the last few years, when he had spoken French to her and told her what was going on in Paris. Altogether, with her rather delicate health, her frequent visits to Edinburgh, and her general insecurity about her own abilities, it was perhaps just as well to put off the business of being mistress of Kintalloch for some time yet. Meg was worried about her uncle's health too, and felt that everything should be done to make his life easy and contented. The presence of his other son would certainly contribute a great deal to this, if he could be persuaded to come.

It wasn't till she was sitting in the Edinburgh train the following day that she made the connexion between getting Angus to come home and the fact that, now and always, he would be the only hope of supplying Kintalloch with an heir. Of course they wanted him to come home. To settle down and marry and have children. That plainly was his duty now, since she had failed them. It was eminently reasonable, and she had to admit that they were being very tactful about it. But that didn't prevent her from feeling desperately hurt. They don't need me now, she thought. Biologically I'm a failure. I know they're all fond of me, and they've all been terribly kind. But they can do without me. I'm superfluous. In fact, I'm a positive hindrance. If I weren't here Gavin could marry again, and they might have a dozen children. He could hardly pick another wife that couldn't give him a child. Most women can have children. I'm the exception, I'm the incompetent one.

That evening Tom announced to his wife and son:

'I've written to Angus. I used all the blandishments I could. We'll see if it works.'

They spoke at length of how useful it would be to have the other brother with them. Nobody mentioned the question of the heir, but Tom did venture to remark that it would be a good thing if he found some nice Scottish lassie and settled down.

'You wouldn't much like it if he brought you home a French daughter-in-law, would you Bessie?'

They all laughed.

'Well,' said Bessie, 'so long as she can speak decent English I don't suppose I'd mind too much. I've forgotten what little French I was taught at school. And I don't have a talent for it, like Meg.'

'Oh, but Meg was taught at home, by a governess,' pointed out Tom.

'Yes, and we all know what came of that,' rejoined Gavin.

There was a silence, broken at last by Bessie. 'Poor Ellen,' she said. 'She's had a hard life, one way and another.'

'She's having a hard life at the moment,' agreed Gavin, 'but I don't think it's been all that bad up till a few months ago. She's never really had much to trouble her. In fact, I think she's had a remarkably easy life up till recently. Look at the way you've worked.'

'I've worked hard from choice. I could have sat in the drawing room all day ordering the servants about, if I'd chosen. I've done what I wanted to do, and my life has been very full. I think Aunt Ellen's life must have been rather empty.'

'Well, perhaps,' conceded Gavin.

Tom was silent.

16

Angus finished reading the letter and put it down on the table. Just then Nancy came into the room, scowling. The thoughtful mood induced by the letter evaporated, and Angus felt his spirits suddenly rising.

'Look!' he exclaimed, waving the letter at Nancy. 'The summons.'

'What summons?' Nancy's scowl deepened.

'From my parents. Come home, be fruitful and multiply, Kintalloch needs an heir.' He jumped up and danced round the room.

Nancy sat down, dissociating herself from his exuberance.

'Is that what they say?'

'Not in so many words. Or rather, not in so few. They take two pages to explain that my father's health isn't good and he's got to take things easy. And it seems the workload is too much for Gavin – who, incidentally, is as strong as an ox and simply loves the work. In fact, I don't suppose he can think of anything else to do. And anyway, there's nothing to keep them from employing someone to run the place.'

'Then why don't they?'

'Tradition. The Lindsays have always run everything themselves. I suppose it's a combination of a sense of duty and a total inability to think of anything else to do with their time.'

'So they want you to go and help?'

'I suppose they do, *en passant*. The important message is written clearly between the lines. If Gavin and Meg can't produce the heir, and we know they can't, then it's up to me. And naturally they would rather have a home-bred heir, with a suitable mother carefully chosen by the whole family, preferably in council.'

'But you're not going, are you?' Nancy was trying not to

sound too anxious. After all, during their last conversation, just before going to bed the previous night, each had threatened to walk out on the other. At the end of the discussion it was not clear who was going to do the walking out, but it was perfectly evident that they weren't, either of them, going to put up with this sort of thing any longer. A sense of the predicament that a walk-out by either would leave Nancy in had clarified matters for her considerably overnight, and the possibility that Angus might accept the family's invitation was most unwelcome to her.

Angus had got up feeling as resentful and bored with the whole situation as when he had gone to bed. It was the usual story. Nancy had been wonderful at first. Then, like all the other women in his life, she had failed to live up to his expectations. Like most of them, she had appealed to him because of her helplessness. She had married a French officer at the end of the war, and in 1919 had come over to join him in Paris. But after only a few months the officer had gone off with someone else. The only contribution he had made towards Nancy's welfare had taken the form of a divorce, after which he had disappeared from her horizon, leaving her penniless. When Angus met her she was living by her wits – which appeared to be not quite sufficient for her needs – ashamed to go back to England and confess her mistake, for she had been solemnly warned by friends and relations against marrying a foreigner.

To Angus she had seemed a forlorn and romantic figure. His sense of chivalry was aroused, and he instantly took her home to share his small flat overlooking the rooftops of Paris. He was doing quite well at the time with his freelance translations and a little teaching, and could afford to be generous.

But as the forlorn element in Nancy's situation decreased, so did the romantic aura in which he had seen her. It wasn't that he expected eternal gratitude – at least, he didn't think that was what he was expecting. But he certainly was not prepared for her frequent fits of bad temper and her generally sluttish behaviour. At this stage he hadn't realized that Nancy was a manic depressive. He began to think it was not so much love as self-interest that kept her so tenaciously at his side.

For her the situation was even simpler. Angus, it seemed, was just the same as any other man. They promised you eternal devotion and then they forgot about you, or grew tired of you. It didn't matter which. In the long run it came to the same thing – they wanted to get rid of you and be free, to start again with someone else, no doubt.

For months things had been getting worse. Time and again they had been about to separate. Then the old passion had flared up again, and they made it up and were happy for a few weeks.

On balance, all the cards were in his favour. The flat was his, and he could earn enough to keep himself in reasonable comfort. She had nothing. No home, no job, no prospects. Curiously enough, it was the knowledge of this inequality that had prevented Angus from breaking loose before now. Even in moments when he was convinced that he felt neither affection nor desire for her, he couldn't completely shrug off a certain sense of responsibility. She had been destitute when they met but this didn't justify him in abandoning her once again to the same helpless state. Now, with the invitation to resume his life at Kintalloch, he felt he had the opportunity he needed. He could break away without the brutality of actually walking out on her, leaving her at least with a roof over her head, even if only provisionally.

'I think,' he said, 'I think I might just go. What about a three months' trial period? That would let me see if I can stand it. And there's a lot to stand, I can tell you. The weather, for one thing. And the isolation. It's not that Kintalloch is at the back of beyond, though it certainly is rural. It's more that I've never known such a hermetic family in my life. They shut themselves off from everything and everyone outside the grounds of the estate. Of course, if you're really badly bitten by the work ethic and a Calvinist sense of duty, what else is there? But I couldn't live like that. If I go we'll have to come to some sort of *modus vivendi*. If they're not prepared to let me spread my nets just a little bit wider, then I'm not staying.'

'And are you thinking of telling them all this? About the three months' trial and the net-spreading?'

'I don't know how much I ought to tell them just yet. I may simply tell them I'll try. That's vague enough, surely? That wouldn't be committing myself to too much.'

'What about me?'

'If you remember, *mon ange*, the one thing we got perfectly clear last night was that we aren't going on like this. I go to Kintalloch, and you have the run of this place, rent free, for the next three months. That will give you quite a long time to look around you, *n'est-ce pas*?'

'Oh, don't talk French to me, you know I hate it.'

'*N'est-ce pas* isn't French, it's international.'

'Well then, don't talk international,' she snapped back. 'What's wrong with plain English?'

'Plain English for plain people, you mean? Oh, come on, don't take that personally,' he added as she made an angry gesture. 'I'm not calling you plain, you know. You're still quite a good-looking dame, after all.'

There were moments when Angus couldn't resist the vicious little dart. Even when trying to mollify her he couldn't help yielding to the childish temptation of putting in the word 'still'. It was a cruel reminder that Nancy was no longer in her first youth. She was well aware that, for a woman in her position, ripeness is very far from all.

Angus spent the rest of the day thinking over the new possibility. Not that he had any real doubts about the advisability of accepting the invitation to go home. The suggestion seemed too good an opportunity of solving the Nancy problem. He just couldn't afford to ignore it. And if he decided to come back at the end of three months and Nancy was still in the flat, well, they would cross that bridge when they came to it.

What he was trying to puzzle out at the moment was just how much of his thinking he ought to tell them at home. It seemed unfair not to let them know that his plans were purely provisional. He didn't want to upset anyone, and it would be nice if he could help the family. On the other hand, he had a strong suspicion that the whole thing would fall to pieces if they realized just how precarious was his commitment to the idea of settling down at Kintalloch. For years he'd thought very little about his family except on the odd occasion when a letter came from home. Then he would think about them all with a mixture of affection and amusement for a few days, or hours, and plunge back into the here-and-now with his customary enthusiasm.

He had been genuinely sorry to hear about Meg's childlessness. Meg had been one of his childhood companions and he was fond of her. He knew too what a blow this must be to Gavin and his parents. But even this regret had been short-lived. There was always something else to do, some work that should have been done days ago, some new play to see, some new battle to fight with Nancy.

He tried to think as little as possible of the change in his own expectations that the lack of an heir might bring about. After all, Gavin was only one year older than he was, and was more than likely to outlive him. If – and it was a big if – he, Angus, were to succeed to the property, he had already thought out what he wanted to do. He would sacrifice himself, but only to the extent of living at Kintalloch most of the year, for he shared his family's scorn of absentee landlords. And he would see to it that he had plenty of long holidays, preferably in Paris, and he would most certainly make sure that somebody competent was engaged to see to the running of the estate. He wasn't going to spend his life with farmers and blacksmiths and gamekeepers.

By late afternoon Nancy was beginning to regret being so snappish with Angus. It really didn't suit her at all that he should go back to Scotland. Having the use of the flat for three months was all very well, but what was to happen to her after that? She had a suspicion that no amount of time would be sufficient to solve her long-term problems. If Angus came back, would he put her out? It might be that a three-month separation would make him feel detached enough to do this. And if he decided to stay on at Kintalloch, he certainly wouldn't keep the flat on indefinitely just for her benefit. It really would be much better if she could persuade him not to go. Once that was settled she was sure she'd be able to make up with him. She needed his financial support, certainly; but she also needed the relationship, stormy as it was.

When Angus came back that evening after his day's teaching, Nancy met him at the door with quite a different expression from her former scowl. He saw at once that she had made an effort with her appearance. The slippers had been replaced by high-heeled sandals, the dressing gown by a slinky dress, and her face was carefully made up. Angus noticed it all and thought:

You needn't have bothered.

Both appeared to have recovered their good humour, and the evening passed pleasantly.

Eventually Nancy asked the question that had been tormenting her all the time:

'Have you thought any more about going back to Scotland?'

'Not much,' he replied.

'Good,' she said. 'I really think you should refuse.'

'I can't do that,' he replied. 'It's too late now.'

'What do you mean?'

'I've already sent a telegram saying they can expect me next week.'

'But you've just said you'd hardly thought about it!'

'That's right. I sent the telegram, so then I stopped thinking about it.'

Nancy wavered between raging and wheedling. In the end her emotions overcame her and she burst into tears. Angus congratulated himself on having sent the telegram before telling her. He was nearly always won over by a woman's tears.

Safe in the knowledge that he was already committed, he comforted her. After all, he pointed out, it was almost certainly only for three months, perhaps even less. He really was only going for the sake of the family. The least he could do was to be seen to try.

But he was sure it wouldn't work.

He was still in the same frame of mind when he got off the train in Edinburgh. The journey was his concession to family solidarity, even though he was persuaded that he could never settle down to the life they had in mind for him. That the visit to Scotland had come at a peculiarly opportune moment in his stormy relationship with Nancy had receded to the back of his consciousness at that point. For the moment he saw himself as the sacrificial victim, and was not greatly prepared to enjoy the role. He had just collected his luggage and was on his way to find out about trains to Kintalloch when he saw Gavin and Meg coming towards him.

'I didn't expect you!' he exclaimed.

'But we expected you! So here we are.' Gavin was evidently delighted to see him. 'He hasn't changed a bit. Has he, Meg?'

'No. Still the same old Angus.'

'And you haven't changed either. Neither of you.'

'I have,' said Meg, who felt that her recent misfortunes had aged her.

'Just a little,' conceded Angus. 'You get prettier and prettier.'

Meg laughed. 'That wasn't what I meant. Don't you think I look older?'

'Perhaps a week or two older. If you're not careful you'll soon begin to look almost grown-up.'

Meg had always been teased by her cousins because she looked much younger than her real age. As a child this had caused her much distress. Now, in her mid twenties, it was no longer a problem. Behind the teasing and the laughing Angus was aware of the anguish that Meg must have gone through. In two years she had changed from looking as if she still ought to be in school uniform, to a thoughtful, rather strained-looking young woman. It was clear she was still grieving over her frustrated motherhood.

Her father's illness and its attendant scandal can't have helped either, reflected Angus.

That night when he went to bed, in the room he had had as a boy, he had to admit that the homecoming had been far pleasanter than he had expected. There was no hint of reproach from any of the family. He was not made to feel like the prodigal son. All of them had given the impression of being grateful to him for coming back, aware that he was giving up the type of life he had chosen for himself. When he thought of his intention of making this a three-month trial, rather than a permanent homecoming, Angus felt a little guilty. Then he thought of Nancy and his assurances that he would almost certainly go back to Paris after the three months. And he wondered where in fact his allegiance ought to lie.

In spite of the self-willed life he had led, Angus was not indifferent to moral values. He had the happy knack of persuading himself that what he wanted to do was the right thing, so few conflicts arose. When they did, as in the present case, he made an earnest, if short-lived, attempt at getting things right.

This time he realized he must reckon with a sense of family. He had, of course, been very aware of the family all the time when he had lived at home, and at intervals since leaving. But that had been a different sort of awareness. Then it was a case of them-out-there: the family, something outside himself, frequently in opposition to his own sense of identity. This time it was very different. For the first time Angus sensed the family as a whole, something that included him, that nourished his sense of identity while enfolding him. He saw it as something strong and continuing, the living link between past and future, and he wanted to belong and contribute to it. He now understood the role of the family in the progress of mankind; not just in the biological sense, as the begetter of new generations, but as the vessel most fitted to carry on traditions and shared values. He went to bed convinced that, however hard it might be to adapt, this was the place destined for him, and he must fill it.

Lying awake, he worried about how to reconcile his duty to his people with his commitment to Nancy. He could, of course, marry Nancy and bring her over here. He was quite sure she would welcome the suggestion. But when he imagined how his family would react to such a woman he decided he'd better give up the idea. She wasn't French, that was in her favour. But the fact that he had picked her up – yes, *picked her up* – in Paris made it nearly as bad. She was as good – or rather, as bad – as foreign.

In addition, Nancy was English. This, by Kintalloch standards, was also just about as bad as foreign.

And quite apart from her nationality and her history, there was her person. All that make-up, the cigarettes, the perfume, the clothes . . .

Oh, my God, the clothes! thought Angus. No well-cut tweeds for Nancy. She really does her best to look like a *demi-mondaine*. And then the fact that she was a divorcee. Never, never, *never* would they accept her – not for the promise of a dozen heirs!

The weeks slipped by remarkably quickly.

Angus had really found the experience less unpleasant than he expected. For the first time in his life he felt part of a team. And when restlessness or boredom threatened, he reminded himself of that sense of family which had so impressed him on the first evening. And so he stuck it out. He realized that, till now, he had lived entirely for himself – and for perhaps a few individuals, always women, whom he had enjoyed protecting and comforting in adversity. But he had missed out on an important and rewarding aspect of life. This corporate effort was a new experience for him, and new experiences always appealed to Angus. He was aware of this, and so hesitated about cutting himself off entirely from Paris and his life there. Sooner or later, he knew, the new situation would no longer be new. Would his recently discovered sense of family be enough then to get him through the difficult patches?

With that doubt in mind he wrote to Nancy saying he would probably be staying on in Scotland. Nancy wrote back saying she had found someone else and would probably have moved out of the flat to join her new lover by the time Angus arrived, if he decided to come back.

He wondered how much of this story to believe.

It might just be bravado, a fairly frequent reaction with Nancy. At any rate, it was nice to think there might not be too much trouble from that quarter.

17

I must tell him, thought Meg. I really *must* have the courage to tell him. If only I can convince him. It would solve so many problems.

For several weeks she had been mulling it over: if she couldn't have a child of her own, why not adopt one? That way Kintalloch *would* have its heir, and Angus needn't feel obliged to marry. Also – and deep down Meg knew that, for her, this was the most important thing – it would give her a child to look after. This would satisfy her thwarted motherhood, and at the same time give her a purpose in life and a position in the household. Unlike Angus, Meg was not an individualist. She had always wanted to be one of a team, and had spent her life feeling rather on the margin. At home in Edinburgh, as a rather isolated only child; and at Kintalloch, as mistress-to-be and mother-to-be. Her time had not yet come; as long as Bessie was in the house, it was Bessie and only Bessie who was the mistress.

As for motherhood, adoption now seemed her only hope. She was tired of her peripheral existence, of having no demands whatever made upon her, as if she herself were still a child. Everybody was kind to her, so kind, but nobody needed her.

When at last she plucked up enough courage to speak to Gavin about her plan, he refused to consider the matter. At first he wouldn't even give any reason for his refusal. But Meg stuck to her guns and kept on demanding a reason.

In the end he said:

'Look, Meg, it's a subject I would much rather not discuss. There's nothing to be gained by it. But if you insist, I'll tell you. First of all, there's Angus. He's given up the life he chose, in order to return here and take his place among us. Now, it's not a thing we've ever discussed, but it would only be reasonable for him to expect that Kintalloch will ultimately go to his child.

I think it would be unfair if we were to cut him out by adopting a child ourselves.'

Meg was thoughtful. 'I hadn't thought of that,' she confessed.

'The other reason is this: when you adopt a child you simply don't know what you are taking on. Heredity is a very powerful factor. I don't like the thought of its being totally unknown. I'd be much happier to think of the next heir as having Lindsay blood in his veins.'

'But suppose Angus *were* to marry,' Meg countered, 'it might be just as bad. You can't tell what the child might inherit from its mother's side.'

'True. But at least we'd know that fifty per cent of it was pure Lindsay blood.'

'And the virtues of Lindsay blood are so potent that satisfaction would be guaranteed, regardless of the other fifty per cent, is that it?' It wasn't often that Meg indulged in waspish remarks, but this was the only way she could mask her present disappointment.

Gavin looked at her helplessly. He had always tried to avoid speaking about the subject of her childlessness, afraid that it would do nothing but upset her, and here was the proof of how right he had been. He felt helpless in the face of the despair he knew she must be feeling.

'Look, Meg,' he said, putting an arm round her waist, 'there's nothing, nothing at all we can do about it. All we can do is try to forget, and just get on with our lives.'

'Forget!' she exclaimed. 'You're lucky if you can forget. I only wish I could.'

'I didn't say I could forget. And I certainly haven't forgotten. But we have to try. It's our only hope.'

Meg was so overwhelmed by her disappointment that she failed to hear the sadness in his voice. She went away feeling that he was asking the impossible of her.

Forget? How could she ever forget? As for getting on with her life, what life had she to get on with? It was all very well for Gavin. His day was occupied; he played an important part in the life around him. Her own role seemed to have shrunk to that of optional ornament. Meg had too serious a cast of mind to be able to accept this without the most bitter mortification.

For days she was so distressed that she spent most of her time avoiding the others, in order to hide her tears. She reflected miserably that this was only possible because she played such an unimportant part in the household that nobody even noticed whether she was there or not. In this she was unfair to Bessie, who could see very well that Meg was upset, but who thought the best she could do was respect the girl's evident wish for solitude, and keep out of her way.

Meg spent a lot of her time these days in the upstairs hall. It was a large, high-ceilinged space, with two big windows looking out to the lawn and beyond that to the glen. During the day this part of the house was usually deserted. Meg liked it for that reason, and also because at one side there was a little recess with a window of its own, also overlooking the glen. Meg spent hours standing at this window, hidden away from the life of the rest of the house.

She was standing there one afternoon, gazing out towards the valley and the plain beyond, unable to see them for the tears in her eyes, when Angus crossed the lawn in front of the house. Looking up he saw Meg at the window, and was struck by the utter desolation revealed by her attitude. On an impulse he turned and went into the house instead of walking on as he had intended. Meg hadn't seen him, but she heard his footsteps as he approached along the hall. She looked round, then turned to the window again to hide her tears.

Angus walked up to her and put an arm round her shoulder, in silence. She was trying to stop the flow of tears and to stifle the sobs that kept rising painfully, making her throat ache.

'Poor Meg,' he said, 'poor, poor Meg.'

Meg gave up her attempt at self-control. She turned round

and laid her head on his shoulder, and sobbed quietly while he stroked her hair.

When the sobbing had ceased she looked up at him and whispered:

'I'm sorry. I know it's very selfish of me.'

Angus took her tear-stained face between his hands and said:

'I don't think you're selfish. It's very natural.' Then he kissed her on the forehead.

She managed a watery little smile.

And then, still holding her face between his hands, he suddenly bent down and kissed her full on the lips.

Meg was too astonished to protest; but she broke loose as soon as she could and fled to her bedroom.

Angus was left surprised at his own action, which had been quite unpremeditated, and wondering whether he had offended her. I'd no right to kiss her like that, he thought, no right whatever. What on earth can she think of me now? Will she be angry enough to tell Gavin? And if she does, what then? Angus was annoyed with himself over his impulsive action, and apprehensive of its possible results. At the same time he couldn't help feeling that life was fundamentally unfair. There had been no dishonourable intention in his mind. All he had felt was an intense desire to comfort this suffering young creature. You're a clumsy idiot all the same, he told himself. All you've done is probably make things even worse for her. And perhaps a good deal worse for yourself into the bargain.

For the next few days Meg appeared to be avoiding him, and he became convinced that he had offended her.

Meg was not offended.

She was indeed avoiding him, as he suspected, but for a very different reason. Her whole world had been turned into chaos by the incident. She had been immensely grateful for his sympathy, and had been greatly comforted by it. Coming after Gavin's stern injunction that she must forget and try to get on with her life, Angus's accepting attitude to her sorrow was unspeakably soothing. He wasn't asking her to be a heroine. And yet he wasn't treating her as if she were a child. He had called her 'poor Meg', not 'poor little Meg'.

Poor little Meg, dear little Meg!

Uncle Tom always referred to her as 'my little girl', and she appreciated the tenderness this implied, but longed to be treated as an equal, an adult among adults. Gavin too, often treated her as a child, it seemed to her – a delightful plaything almost, to be petted and humoured and, on occasion, reprimanded and told she must try harder, as had happened the other day when she had raised the subject of adoption.

Here at last was someone who treated her as an equal, as a grown woman, with the right to a woman's sorrows. All this was confirmed by the nature of that second kiss. Every time she thought of that kiss and all that it might imply, she felt weak with surprise and expectation. And yet she had to keep on reminding herself that he had no right to kiss her like that. A kiss, she knew, one single kiss, was an immensely powerful force. She remembered the sense of being on the brink of a new world that she had felt when Gavin had kissed her hand that day all those years ago, before going off to the war. Now she felt this other kiss was going to have the same cataclysmic effect on her life. Even if she never saw Angus again, something had happened that could not be undone. It had set off a whole train of feelings that had to be reckoned with. It had presented her with the possibility of an option – a forbidden one, true, but an option all the same. For once she was in the position of being able to make a choice.

If she followed the path of duty she could either let him see that he had behaved badly, or else ignore the situation – which would probably be just as effective. She knew she ought to follow one of these courses, but she couldn't make up her mind to renounce the sort of comfort that Angus had offered her. She was uncertain, apprehensive and excited. Not an easy state of mind to live in, but preferable to the numb misery that seemed to have become her permanent lot. To have anything as positive as a dilemma in her life was a big improvement.

She was still undecided as to what she ought to do, or what she wanted to do – which didn't seem to be the same at all – when Angus came into the library one day when she was sitting there trying to read. Her thoughts had been so entirely bound up with him that she hadn't noticed him coming in, and was quite startled to see him standing in front of her.

Angus interpreted her evident perturbation as a proof that he had offended her.

'Don't run away, Meg, please,' he pleaded. 'I've only come to apologise.'

Meg shook her head. 'I don't want an apology,' she said.

'Please Meg, don't let it spoil things between us. I know how angry you must be, but . . . '

Again she shook her head. 'I'm not angry,' she said. She had edged her way round the table so that now she stood between him and the door. With a little darting movement towards him, she stood on tiptoe and whispered in his ear:

'I liked it,' then turned and ran out of the room.

Those three words completely undermined all Angus's honourable intentions. He had come prepared to apologise, to promise that it would never happen again, and also – just to make sure it didn't – to keep out of her way as much as possible.

So what was he to do now?

Angus had a feeling that perhaps the best solution might be the first train for Paris. But how could he abandon poor Meg after she had made such a confession? He wondered whether he ought to speak to Gavin, to try and persuade him to show a little more sympathy towards his wife. If only he weren't so bloody British, thought Angus. Can't he see that Meg needs something a bit gentler than a stiff upper lip?

It was now his turn to agonize over what line of action he

ought to follow, while Meg waited in trepidation, wondering what on earth he must think of her.

Two days later she found out, when he found her waiting in the recess. More kisses were exchanged, and a promise to meet in the woods further up the glen.

Meg couldn't believe she was behaving like this. She felt as if she were living someone else's life. This was the most exciting thing that had ever happened to her, but she was dogged by a sense of unreality, as if it were all something she had imagined. She knew she was perilously near to adultery, and yet she could do nothing to stop herself. Each meeting with Angus was to be the last, and yet inevitably it was followed by another.

Angus had reached one of the recurrent periods in the course of his life when he simply abandoned himself to events. He was far from happy about these secret meetings with his brother's wife; but how could he break loose without hurting poor Meg terribly? Perhaps it was wishful thinking on his part, but it seemed to him that Meg's need of help and tenderness was paramount. If the process of giving Meg the tenderness she needed happened to be a remarkably pleasant one, that was just one of those things. And anyway, he was paying for his pleasure by his awareness of the danger of the situation, and the fact that it could not possibly go on for long.

Meanwhile, he allowed himself to drift, leaving any initiative to Meg or to circumstances. For he was well aware that – in a small, inward-looking household like theirs – the possibility of discovery was ever present. Well, when that happened, the situation would resolve itself.

This gentle side of Angus that had come to light was a revelation to Meg. She had always known him as lively, impulsive, headstrong, sometimes even cruel with his capacity for biting sarcasm. The tenderness that her misery had evoked in him was something totally unexpected. As a child it had always been Gavin she had run to for protection and consolation when things went wrong. Up till now any comparisons she had made between the two brothers had always been in Gavin's favour. She admired his strength and serenity, his ability to cope with adversity. She had never known him say anything intended to hurt, either out of anger or for the sake of a *bon mot*. Ever since their marriage the only fault she had been able to find in him was his tendency to treat her rather like a child.

Now, compared with his brother, Gavin seemed to Meg rather dull and stodgy, incapable of flights of fancy or unexpected reactions. She admitted to herself that her husband seemed a rather monochrome character. He certainly didn't scintillate. For the first time she realized her need of a little sparkle to brighten the dull monotony of her existence. Even a bout of bad temper would have been a relief. But Gavin was always equable and reasonable. She told herself that to reproach him with this was eminently unreasonable. She was being unfair to him, in her thoughts and in her actions. In short, she decided, she wasn't good enough to be his wife. Not only could she not give him the children he wanted, but she was unfaithful to him in her heart, and not even wholly faithful to him in her actions.

And yet she could not give up Angus and the tenderness he offered her. She felt she simply could not contemplate going back to her previous comfortless state. For days there seemed to be no possible solution. Then one morning a luminous idea came to her. At first it seemed so radical that she was doubtful about how to broach the subject even with Angus.

But that same afternoon it was Angus, in one of his sudden bursts of self-reproach, who gave her the very opening she was looking for.

'It's no good, Meg,' he said when they met in the wood, 'we can't go on like this. I have absolutely no right to go on seeing you in this way. Besides, I'm beginning to wonder whether my mother suspects something.'

'Why? Has she said anything?'

'No. But I just see her looking at me – in a sort of thoughtful way. It's not like her not to say what's on her mind. It must be something she considers pretty serious. So I've made up my mind. We must put an end to this before there's some terrible explosion. I could never forgive myself if I involved you in that.'

'What do you mean to do?'

'I must go back to Paris. I don't know what excuse I can give. I'll have to think of something. But going back to Paris is the only way out.'

To his surprise Meg looked at him with sparkling eyes. 'Yes,' she said, 'Paris is the answer.'

He couldn't understand it. He had expected tears and reproaches and pleas for him to stay. Instead, she seemed delighted. 'You don't mind?' he asked, feeling rather foolish.

'No, of course I don't mind. I'll come with you.'

Angus was appalled.

From every point of view this would be a disaster. He had said nothing to Meg, or to any other member of the family, about Nancy. And Nancy was very probably in his flat at this very minute. He hadn't been at all convinced by the story of the new lover. So, as far as Meg was concerned, her arrival in Paris, with the discovery of Nancy in his flat, would completely shatter the dream-world she had been living in. As for the rest of the family, he couldn't bear to think of what this would mean to them. His involvement with Meg had cut across the sense of family that had been with him since his arrival, but it had done nothing to diminish it. He realized that by his action he had forfeited his right to his proper place in the family; but he regretted this bitterly, and hoped to shield Gavin and his parents from the consequences of his irresponsible behaviour.

He was staring at Meg in silence, perplexed and unhappy. Oh, God, he thought, what sort of a mess have I got myself into? What on earth can I say to her?

Meg stared back, in growing disquiet. 'You don't want me to come?' she said at last, very quietly.

'Oh, Meg, darling Meg, of course I want you to come. But it's quite impossible. Have you thought of what we would be doing to Gavin if you came away with me? So far our only justification, if you can call it that, has been that we meant to keep this secret, that Gavin would never know. But you can't keep it secret when a man's wife runs away with another man – and his own brother, at that. Think of the scandal of it. Don't you think we've had enough scandal in the family as it is?'

Meg had heard nothing of the old story of the supposed incest. She thought he was referring to her father's only too public affair with another woman.

She sighed. 'I know,' she said, 'but at least that wasn't a Lindsay affair. Your family can hardly be blamed for my father's misdemeanours.'

Only then did Angus realize that Meg had probably heard nothing of the incest story. It had all happened many years ago, of course; but the ugly rumours were still repeated from time to time. What an odd family we are, he thought. So close, so turned in upon ourselves, and yet so silent with each other. He had heard the rumours when he was at school, and several times on more recent occasions, but he had never spoken of them in the family, not even to his brother. Was it possible that Gavin had said nothing about it to Meg? Or perhaps he himself hadn't heard them.

This misunderstanding of Meg's put Angus in a serious predicament. He either had to let her think he had made a very insensitive allusion to her father, or else tell her the truth about the scandal he was referring to. He decided he would have to leave things as they were. This was hardly the moment to reveal so serious an accusation against her own mother.

'Well, let's forget about the other scandal,' he said. 'There would be quite enough in this one, if we were to go off together. Can't you see what it would do to Gavin?'

Meg laughed. 'Can't *you* see that it would be the very best thing we could do for Gavin?'

'Frankly, no,' he said, wondering whether the tension of the last few days had been too much for Meg's mental balance. 'I can't see that losing you would do anything for Gavin except drive him to despair. He loves you. Surely you know that?'

'Of course I know that. I'm his child-wife and he's very fond of me. But that's not the most important thing, not in his life, anyway. Kintalloch comes first. If I run away with you he can divorce me and marry someone else who can give him a child. Can't you see how perfectly it would all work out?'

18

Come, love, and still the asking in my heart
Come, love, with love to comfort my desiring
And let me feel your throbbing heart on mine
And all your pulses beating in my blood.
Time or satiety will kill our passion
Though your mouth speak to mine of endless bliss
And though your lips bruise mine to prove the strength
Of our insistent lust, yet this will die.
Accept this transitoriness and let
Soul speak to soul through body's ecstasy.
So let us take love gladly, knowing this:
From the dead grain springs forth the living corn.

Ellen read her poem yet again, puzzling over the two missing lines. She had started off with the intention of writing an unrhymed sonnet, but the two middle lines of the sestet eluded her.

Let earth and sea and sky and all creation
Incessantly proclaim, These two have loved.

Hmm, she thought, that's not bad. But obviously that has to be the last couplet. It's a summation of what has gone before. And so, of course, is the couplet I've already got at the end. It has to stay there. So, what I've got is a sonnet, with the requisite fourteen lines, only the last two pairs are incompatible. That means I can either leave it at twelve lines, and forget about writing a sonnet, or struggle on till I find the two missing lines.

Then another possibility struck her.

She could write two sonnets on the same subject – a whole sonnet sequence, if she felt like it – since she now had the endings for two. She thought about this for some time, then decided she didn't want to write even one more sonnet on the same subject. She was beginning to feel that perhaps she had now written enough about her passionate love affair. Funny, she thought, if anyone who knows me were to read this they would think I was writing about Donald. And then she remembered all the old rumours, and wondered whether some people might after all suspect the truth.

No, she decided, she couldn't possibly think of trying to publish this one, or any of the other love poems.

That was another reason for moving away from this type of poetry. As practice gave her confidence she grew more and more attracted to the thought of publishing, some time in the future. Life had settled into a fairly calm routine. She knew that her afternoons with Donald might go on for years, but that there was no possibility of a return to normal life for him. So she was on her own most of the day, except for Meg's visits. She had all the time in the world, and felt she wanted a fixed purpose in her life. The accumulation of enough poems for the inevitably slim volume would give her life the direction it lacked. And if publication was to be the aim, then no more love poems, no more deeply personal introspection. She would branch out into something quite different, both in content and form.

And the poems she started writing now were indeed different. The form was less structured, and the love theme had disappeared. But they were still deeply personal and introspective. The anguish remained, a retrospective anguish. She relived all the misery of the past as she wrote, but afterwards felt cleansed and relieved.

Nothing has been achieved.
The path you followed, so convinced
that you walked straight,
clung to earth's curve
and it has brought you back

134

to where you started from.
How often now have you been here before?

And why set off again?
The path you followed,
followed once again,
will lead you here again and nowhere else.
And here –
you know what that is,
stale and bleak and bare
and unendurably the same,
and always and entirely you.
L'enfer, c'est pas les autres,
c'est toi-même.

This hell you are,
must it remain the same?
Can nothing alter, nothing mitigate
the fact of being what you are?
Must every path lead back to consciousness of this?

Some day perhaps you'll find another path,
Some divine tangent that will lead away
and not curve back to where you started from.

She decided she would call that one 'Circle'. Or perhaps it should be 'Tangent'. That would emphasize the positive side of it. But perhaps too much?

Some of her time spent sitting beside Donald was occupied by her poetry. She made a point of never actually writing anything while she was with him. But the silence and stillness left her mind free to follow its own bent, and the poetry was, at this stage of her life, the dominant factor in her thought.

* * *

Mornings were perhaps the easiest time.

Walking over to the hospital, talking to Donald, reading to Donald, then walking home again. All these activities gave pattern and purpose to that part of the day. It was after lunch that Matilda became most aware of the blank that Donald's illness had left in her life. During the years of their association Donald's evening visits had shaped her whole day, even the days when she knew he wasn't coming. There was always something to be done for his next visit – shopping to do, something special to prepare in the kitchen, a book to read that he had recommended, a little extra care with the housework so that everything would look warm and welcoming when he arrived. Now, after her visit to the hospital the whole structure of the day seemed to crumble. There was no point in cooking anything special, no point in raiding her little garden for flowers to put on the table. No point in anything, really. After today's visit was over there seemed to be nothing to look forward to – except the same sad routine tomorrow.

Matilda was grateful to Martin Carr for the suggestion that there might be something left in Donald capable of 'advancing', as he had put it. This meant that, if there was any consciousness at all left, she could perhaps help him, however minimally, on his journey. So she kept on holding his hand and stroking his face, and talking and reading aloud to him, and reciting poetry. She had a great store of poems in her memory, and he used to enjoy listening to her reciting them, admiring both her memory and the vivid way she brought the poem to life.

'I don't know how you do it,' he would say. 'I've never been able to remember as much as two lines of poetry. And yet I've always liked it so much.'

'Your head's too full of those terrible legal terms,' she would answer, laughing.

Now, after greeting him, she would sit down and tell him all the minutiae of the day, down to the most insignificant detail; a new rose in bloom, a broken milk bottle, the sudden gust of wind that had nearly blown her hat away. And then she would take out her book and read to him, or else suggest some poetry.

'How about Browning? We both like Browning. Let's have "My Last Duchess". I think I can remember the whole of it.'

So Donald spent the final years of his life in the presence of poetry, the unwritten poems which his wife was forging silently at his bedside, and the well known and much loved poems which his lover recited to him. The nurses shook their heads over the behaviour of the two women.

'One of them sitting silent as a mummy, never utters a word, and the other talk, talk, talking all the time. I bet the poor man never got a word in edgeways, with that one.'

19

Gavin slept well that night, though he hadn't expected to, for Meg had gone to bed very early with a terrible headache, and looking so ill that he had been worried. He had, in fact, been worried about her for some time, she seemed so far away and disengaged from everything that was going on. He wondered whether she was going to sink into the sort of passive indifference that seemed to have possessed her mother for as long as he could remember. He went to bed expecting to find her awake and restless; but she appeared to be sleeping peacefully, and he lay down beside her feeling somewhat reassured, and soon fell asleep.

Meg was only pretending to be asleep so as not to have to speak to Gavin. In fact, she spent the whole night awake, in a state of utter indecision. Angus had refused even to consider the possibility of letting her go to Paris with him. She knew he meant to steal out of the house at some point during the night, leaving behind a note for his father with some excuse, though he didn't know yet what. Meg had to yield to his refusal to take her with him, but she still could not accept their parting as final.

Suppose she got up and preceded him to the station? Surely he couldn't refuse to take her with him, especially if she had left a note for Gavin telling him this was what she had done? Sometimes she managed to persuade herself that she would indeed do this. It was just a case of waiting till the whole household was asleep. Then she would walk the three miles to the station and just wait for him to turn up. At other times she felt sure he wouldn't go away, that he would still be there in the morning, and that they would go on seeing each other as before. Then this hope would fade, leaving only the bleak certainty of separation, and she would lie rigid, hardly daring to breathe, listening for any sound that would indicate his departure.

She heard nothing, and when morning came she could hardly bear to wait till the household was up and about, in order to find out whether he had indeed gone. Ill as she felt, she got up and reached the breakfast table before anyone else. She looked at the place laid for Angus, with the silver napkin ring resting on the table, just as on any ordinary day. In spite of her conviction that he must have gone she found herself praying that he would come in and sit down, that she would see his hand pick up the napkin and take it out of its ring.

Soon Bessie and Gavin came in. When Bessie asked her whether her headache had gone she said yes, she was all right. But she looked so ill, and her voice sounded so lifeless that Gavin and his mother exchanged a sceptical look.

'Well, let's sit down, anyway,' said Bessie. 'I don't know where those two have got to. Not very punctual, you men, are you?' she said to Gavin.

'I am. On time for breakfast, as usual. Ever known me be late for a meal?'

They were both doing their best to keep the conversation going while they waited, aware of the distress that Meg was trying so hard to hide. She was now certain that Angus must have gone, and that Tom's delay was caused by his having received the farewell letter. She wanted desperately to run away, to her bedroom, anywhere, not to be there when the news was broken. Yet, at the same time, she could not bear the suspense of not knowing what had happened. And so she sat on, waiting.

At last Tom came in. It was clear from his expression that he was extremely upset. He had a letter in his hand, which he was trying to hold steady, but with little success.

'What is it, Tom?' Bessie got up and hurried over to her husband.

'It's Angus. He's gone. Back to Paris, it seems. Here, read it.'

'Aloud?'

'You might as well. We've all got to know. Everyone else will have to know too.'

Bessie sat down at her place and read the letter in a steady voice.

In the midst of her anguish Meg couldn't help noticing the control this woman was able to exercise. How can she, how can she! she thought. Her son has just walked out on the whole family, and she can sit there reading the letter without a tremor!

'My dearest Father,' read Bessie, 'By the time you get this I shall be well on my way to Paris. I have no excuse. I can hardly even apologise. The only explanation I can give is that I have realized, irrevocably, that I cannot fit into the life of Kintalloch as we all would have wished. It's simply a case of a square peg in a round hole. I did try, in all earnestness, and for a time I thought I could do it. Now I see that I can't, and the only honourable thing is to go, without arguments or recriminations. I am sure that, in the course of time, you will all find you can get on very well without me. I am sorry, I am truly sorry for the pain that I know this must cause you. I love you all. Angus.'

Nobody spoke, nobody moved. The longer the silence lasted, the more difficult it became for anyone to break it. At last Meg burst into tears, got up and ran out of the room. She felt she had to be alone or die.

Before she reached the stairs Gavin had caught up with her.

'No,' she said, 'no. Go back to your parents. They need you.'

Nothing else would have persuaded Gavin to leave her at that moment, she knew.

Two days later Meg was still in bed, feverish and complaining of a terrible headache. Against her will the doctor was sent for. She had little faith that medicine could do anything for her, knowing only too well what her real complaint was. One of her miseries was constant worry whether any of the others suspected her involvement in Angus's sudden departure. If they did they certainly didn't show it. But then, that was what the family was like. Both here and at home in Edinburgh, she was used to this wall of silence about the important things. Apart from her mother, who was predominantly silent all the time, the others were all quite chatty about the things that didn't matter. Bessie in particular prattled on most of the time. But seldom about the important things, and never about the things that hurt, a reticence she had learned soon after her entry into the family.

The two men were out when Doc arrived, and Bessie met him in the hall.

'Well, Bessie, what have you done with the patient? Hidden her away, eh?'

Bessie kissed her father.

'No, she's in bed. She wanted to get up today, but we thought she was too feverish.'

'And I hear that young scamp of a grandson of mine has run off again. The black sheep of the family, that's what he is, and I say it myself, grandson or no grandson. Just a black sheep. Leaving you all in the lurch like that.'

Doc didn't share the Lindsay tendency to silence on important issues.

'What took him, eh? That's what I want to know. What took him?'

'Square peg in a round hole, Dad. He thought he could adjust, but then found he couldn't. We're all very sad about it, and I think it's all been too much for Meg. She hadn't really recovered properly from the loss of the child, you know.'

'I know, I know. It's a sad time for you all. Well, I'll go up and see the patient. No, you needn't come with me. I know my way. Remember I knew my way about this house long before you ever set foot in it.'

Bessie knew her father had a way with young people, and hoped he might win Meg's confidence. Not that she expected Doc to pass on anything he had learned. She knew this would not happen. But she felt sure it would help Meg if she could tell her trouble to someone sympathetic. She herself, Bessie, had a pretty good idea of what that trouble was. She had been surprised and hurt by Angus's sudden departure, but she had been convinced for some time that the problem existed. She just wished he could have found some sort of solution that was less hurtful to them all. And she realized that the solution had to come from Angus. Meg, she suspected, was too immature to be anything but a pawn in the game.

Poor Bessie, who had unquestioningly accepted the family ethic of silence, would dearly have loved to be able to talk the matter over with someone. But it was a matter that had to be kept within the family, so that narrowed down the possibilities. She couldn't discuss it with her father because of his position as doctor and confessor. And she was afraid to mention it to Tom or Gavin, in case they suspected nothing. If that were the case they were best left in ignorance. That leaves only Ellen, she thought. But I never see her now that she visits Donald every day in hospital. Besides, she's not an easy person to approach at the best of times, and I don't see myself going up to her and saying:

'I think your daughter is having an affair with my younger son.'

Bessie sighed and decided that the only thing for it was to go and see how the maids were getting on with giving the pantry its spring-clean. Keep busy, she thought. Just keep busy, and it will all sort itself out.

'Well, young woman!' Doc stood in the doorway and surveyed his patient. 'I suppose you want me to tell you what's the matter with you, eh? Or are you going to tell me?'

Meg muttered something about a headache and feeling feverish.

'Oh, I know all that, I know all that. The real problem is what's causing it. And as I don't suppose you know, I'll tell you what it is. Oh, yes. I can tell, just standing in the doorway here, without as much as taking your pulse. I know what's wrong. You're suffering from a bad attack of youth, that's what it is. Am I right?'

Meg shook her head and tried to smile.

'You think not, eh? You think you know better. Ah, but I'll

stick to my diagnosis all the same. Youth, my dear, youth, that's all that's the matter with you.'

He shut the door and advanced into the room, shaking his head, then sat down on the bed. 'And if you don't believe me, just answer this one question. Would you be grieving like this – for I can see that you are grieving – would you be in this situation if you were my age? Seventy-nine, that is. More than fifty years older than you are.'

This time Meg actually managed a faint smile and shook her head.

'There you are, you see? That's what it is. Just a bad case of youth. A very prevalent affliction. But the one thing to be said for it is that it's self-limiting. Just leave it long enough and it cures itself. Now, I know you've had a very difficult time, losing your three babies, and everything else. It's not surprising that you're a bit down. I'll give you a prescription for a bottle. The other thing you need doesn't require a prescription. It comes free, and is readily available. It's called time, and there's plenty of it.'

'Time passes very slowly,' Meg remarked.

'Don't you believe it, my dear, don't you believe it.'

Gavin too had his suspicions, though these had only formed after Angus's departure. He remembered how upset Meg had been the evening before Angus left, and how strangely she had been behaving for some time before that. Seeing her obvious distress, on the morning after Angus had left, suddenly made him realize the probable explanation. He was hurt, uncertain and angry, but couldn't quite decide who to be angry with. Angus, presumably. But still, he felt certain that his brother had not deliberately tried to steal his wife's affection from him. Meg he still thought of as too immature for him to blame her fully.

In the end he came to the conclusion that perhaps he ought to blame himself. He must have failed Meg in some way for her to feel the temptation to get involved with Angus. He wished they could speak about it, so that he could find out where he had gone wrong, if indeed that was where the root of the matter lay. But he was afraid to raise the subject in case Meg should think he was reproaching her. He wondered whether his mother suspected anything. He would have liked to ask her, but felt he couldn't do so without betraying a lack of confidence in Meg.

The only person who had no suspicion of the truth was Tom. From his position of total ignorance, Angus's departure without consultation or even a word of farewell seemed utterly unjustifiable, and he wondered that Bessie and Gavin should show so little resentment.

It's all very well to talk about square pegs and round holes, he thought. Didn't I give up my career to come home and help my father? No question of square pegs then. You do your duty, and that pares off the sharp edges. The peg, after all, can be made to fit the hole. Angus just didn't try. I wonder whether he's got some sort of entanglement in Paris. That would explain it. And I don't care what Bessie says – after all, she's his mother, therefore partial. I think he's let us all down badly.

20

He's a bugger, thought Nancy. A selfish, unreliable, unpredictable bugger. *I* don't want him back, *I* don't need him for anything. Except, perhaps, the flat. Not that it's up to much, anyway. Even at its best.

Looking around her, Nancy had to admit that it certainly wasn't looking anything like its best just at that moment. She had made virtually no effort to clean it since Angus had left months ago. Clothes, most of them dirty, were lying about on the chairs, on the table, even on the floor; and along with the clothes were dirty plates, cups, cutlery, and several saucepans. The dressing table and the window-sills were littered with bottles, jars and tubs of make-up, most of them half-used, without their tops. There were also newspapers, paper bags, and here and there an empty gin-bottle.

Now that she was properly awake and had dragged herself out of the bed, the usual daily problem presented itself. How was she going to spend the day? Had she enough money for food – and drink? She opened her purse and examined the contents. Just enough for a bottle of gin, or some food. Not both. Perhaps she ought to go and do some work. A few hours at the sink of the café round the corner would produce enough for a decent meal. Nancy didn't know whether she could be bothered. But she'd have to get dressed, anyway, even if only to go out and buy the gin.

She went into the bedroom.

I ought to change the sheets, she thought, looking at the filthy bed. I haven't changed them since he went away, and they were none too clean even then. Perhaps there was a clean pair somewhere. Or perhaps not. She couldn't remember. She had a faint recollection of pawning some sheets a few weeks ago, but she hadn't been particularly sober at the time and perhaps she'd only thought about it without getting round to it. She shrugged her shoulders and lit a cigarette.

Half an hour later she was on her way up the stairs again, with a bottle sticking out of her pocket. She had decided against work. She just wasn't feeling up to it today. She had nearly made up her mind to spend the money on food, then reflected that she would be just as hungry tomorrow as well as being miserable all day today. Better to get some drink and enjoy her day. Once you're drunk enough you don't notice the hunger, she reminded herself. As she climbed the stairs she heard the concierge shouting something to her. All she could make out was the word 'merdeuse'. Must have seen the bottle sticking out of my pocket, she thought. Things had been easier long ago. She remembered her grandmother going home with a bottle in her pocket. But with all those yards and yards of skirt nobody knew about the bottle. Eased down into that deep, capacious pocket, it disappeared completely. She wondered now whether everybody had such deep pockets in those days, or perhaps this was a special stratagem of her grandmother's.

She was a deep one, she was, thought Nancy with a chuckle, I wouldn't put it past her to make those pockets specially deep for you-know-what.

It was late that night when Angus got back. He felt sure he would find Nancy in residence, and wondered what to tell her. He knew she could be both coarse and unfair, and hesitated to give her the chance to judge Meg according to her own standards. On the other hand, on one of her good days, Nancy could be both sensitive and compassionate. Perhaps he would risk telling her. He longed to talk the whole matter over at length, to justify Meg, to justify himself.

As he reached the top landing he saw a thin light beneath the door. When he got in he thought Nancy must have gone to bed leaving the light on. The room seemed empty. Then he noticed her, sprawled over the one easy chair, fast asleep.

The half empty bottle and the smell of gin made the situation perfectly clear. God! he thought, this is what I've come back to. He stood looking at her coarsened features, her dirty clothes and her abandoned attitude, and he thought of Meg with her delicate features, her fine skin and her thoughtful, timid expression. For a moment he thought he simply wouldn't be able to spend the night in the flat. But the alternative was to walk the streets of Paris, and he realized he was too tired. He had been travelling since early morning and hadn't slept at all the previous night. He decided he would just have to put up with things as they were, and throw Nancy out the following morning.

Meanwhile, he was very hungry.

In the kitchen he found nothing but chaos, so he went back to the sitting room. There seemed to be nothing for it but to follow Nancy's example. He tipped one of the chairs over to get rid of all the stuff piled on it, picked up the bottle and put it to his lips. There was no point in looking for a glass; he knew he wouldn't find one. He sat and drank till the combination of misery, hunger, exhaustion and alcohol got the better of him, and he let himself slide on to the floor and fall asleep.

When Angus woke up it was daylight, and Nancy had disappeared. Probably gone for more drink, he thought, since I finished off her bottle. I suppose I'd better get up. Can't lie on the floor all day. But he felt too tired and aching and headachy to make the effort. The floor, after all, seemed a not uncomfortable place to be. Then he noticed that a rug had been thrown over him and a pillow placed under his head.

Gratefully he closed his eyes and let himself sink back into sleep.

21

Slowly Meg began to drag herself out of the apparently bottom-less pit of her misery. She had not had the slightest intention of telling Doc anything at all, but found herself telling him nearly everything. The bit about her idea of running away with Angus, with the rationalisation about getting a divorce so that Gavin could marry again, she held back. She was already beginning to think this a piece of childish wishful thinking on her part. But telling Doc the rest of the story had not only brought the relief of confession, but also the practical advantage of reassuring her about any suspicions the rest of the family might have had. She asked him point-blank whether he thought they had seen or suspected what was going on.

Doc had a pretty good idea that Bessie at least must have had an inkling. But he summoned all his professional *sang froid,* and lied heroically.

Meg was immensely relieved.

Gradually her strength came back and she resumed normal life. Sadder than before, but perhaps less bored. At first this was purely because she had been through a most interesting experience, in which she had played a central part. The outcome had been sad and, indeed, mortifying. She knew she was very much to blame. But at the same time, sorrow and self-blame, while hard to deal with, were at least something there, something to be reckoned with, something that saved her from the endless vacuum in which she had seemed to be living. The thought that she had been within a hair's breadth of becoming 'a fallen woman', as she put it, was astonishing, frightening and immensely interesting. She knew that, in private at least, she qualified for the description of 'a woman with a past', and she took some satisfaction in this, while at the same time feeling immensely relieved that it was not public knowledge.

During her last tormented meeting with Angus he had tried to make her realize the sort of treatment that would be meted out to her if she put herself in this position. She had paid little attention at the time, and refused to accept his arguments. Now she was beginning to see how right he had been and that she, of all people, was totally unfitted to stand up to the slights, disparagement and insults that her position would have called forth. She recognized that 'young Mrs Lindsay of Kintalloch' had led too protected a life to be able to cope with anything less than the respect she had always taken for granted.

Angus wrote occasionally to his parents – brief, uninformative letters, designed merely to keep them from worrying about him. In spite of their disappointment in him he knew that their affection was stronger than their sense of injury, and that there was no question of anything like a final break between him and the family. He told them he had gone back to his teaching and translating, and that there was nothing else new to report. His tempestuous liaison with Nancy continued, but that was neither new nor to be reported. His parents sometimes suspected that there might be a woman in his life, but they only suspected it on principle, as it were, having no specific information on the matter.

And then one day, about six months after his return to France, his parents received a long and most informative letter. In it Angus said that he had formed a liaison with an English girl living in Paris – he omitted to mention the fact that this had been going on for years already. He was telling them this, which he knew must grieve them, because he had just learned that they were to have a child.

'Normally, I know,' he went on, 'you would expect me to marry the girl, and this I am prepared to do. But before I commit myself to this course of action I must tell you that she is in all respects the sort of woman you would consider quite unfit to be your daughter-in-law. Her background is very different from ours; she smokes and swears and, on occasion, drinks too much.

In addition, she is a divorcee. I am telling you all this not out of disloyalty to her but because you have a right to know what sort of woman I am contemplating bringing into the family. And I am thinking of marrying her not so much for her own sake, or even for the sake of the child, as because in this way I can make some sort of reparation to you for my failure to take my place in the family, by providing it with a legitimate heir. If you wish to acknowledge this child as a member of the family, I promise that, as soon as it is old enough to go to boarding school, it shall be sent to England, and can from then on look on Kintalloch as its home.'

Anger, dismay, outrage, hope, curiosity, incredulity, all these struggled for supremacy in the perplexed family. They held a council of war and tried to decide what to say to Angus. They decided on one thing, only to change their collective mind a minute later. At one moment it was clear that the whole thing was a tragedy but that Angus must marry the girl on moral grounds. At another it was equally clear that no such marriage could be entertained, no, not even on moral grounds. The whole thing was just too distasteful. And who but Angus would ever come up with such a hare-brained idea!

Then there were the claims of the child, the poor little innocent. And then the fear that the child might turn out like its mother, a bad lot. And so on, with most of them adopting every contradictory position in turn.

Meg sat silent, as usual in family council. But the more she thought of it, the more she longed for them to decide in favour of accepting the child into the family. For, of course, it would be she and Gavin who acted the part of mother and father to the infant.

The argument went on and on, not acrimonious, but bewildered and perturbed. Meg woke up from a dream of surrogate motherhood to hear Gavin say something about heredity.

'You just don't know what such a child might inherit from its mother.'

And Meg spoke.

'But with fifty per cent Lindsay blood,' she said, looking archly at her husband, 'that should make it all right.'

Gavin looked at her in surprise, then realized she was quoting his very own words, as spoken during their discussion of a possible adoption. He smiled and nodded, to show he had recognized the reference.

At least he knew now quite clearly what Meg was hoping for. Since Angus's departure Gavin had tried very hard to see things from Meg's point of view, suspecting that he had lost her affection and must do all he could to win it back again.

Meg felt her hour had come.

'Besides,' she pointed out, 'whether we like it or not, that child is going to be a Lindsay, the rightful heir of Kintalloch. Do you really want one of the family to be brought up in such deplorable circumstances, disowned by his family for no fault of his own?'

Gavin, now sure of his ground where Meg was concerned, supported her view. Suddenly they were all in agreement. Angus was to marry the girl, and the child was to take its place in Kintalloch as soon as it was old enough. They then started a sort of sub-argument as to how soon that would be – which Tom cut short with the comment:

'Well, not before the child is born, anyway.'

It was meant as a joke, and they took it as such. But as the little meeting broke up Tom realized that his remark could be taken in another sense, namely, that there was no place for the mother in Kintalloch.

It's not what I meant when I said it, he thought, but it's true all the same. Whatever happens, that woman's not coming here. I'm not having Bessie and Meg dealing with a woman like that.

At first Meg was terribly excited at the thought of having the child to look after. But as things settled back to routine again she forced herself to accept that it would be years – seven or eight, or even longer – before the child came. It was going to make no immediate difference to her life. And then the thought struck her that the next few years would enable her to prepare for motherhood. With my own babies, she thought, perhaps I was too young. I'll be able to make a better job of it now, when the time comes.

22

Nancy did not enjoy her pregnancy. She wasn't even looking forward to motherhood, and missed no occasion of making this clear to Angus.

'It's a pity you can't have the child instead of me,' she remarked one day. 'It's you and your damn family that want it.'

Angus usually tried to calm these outbursts with sympathy and hopeful words. This time, thinking of Meg and her desperate longing for motherhood, he snapped back:

'Some women would sell their soul to be able to have a child.'

'Well, I'd rather have an abortion any day.'

Angus wasn't exactly looking forward to parenthood either, not in the present circumstances. He often wondered whether he had been wise in offering the child to Kintalloch. Perhaps they would all have been better to let Nancy have her abortion. But once again the ghost of that feeling of family, of pride in the continuation of the race, came to him, silencing his doubts. Besides, there was Meg. This child was meant for the family, but most especially for Meg. He knew she would look upon it as her own. All her longing for motherhood would at last find fulfilment.

'It's too late now to think about an abortion,' he said.

'Yes, and whose fault is that? All those weeks saying you couldn't raise the money, and all the time you were plotting with your family.'

'Don't let's go over all that again. You've got something out of it too – a wedding ring and an assured future. No more hours standing washing dishes in that stinking café. You could even go back into respectable society if you behaved a little less like a slut. But that obviously means nothing to you.'

'Respectable! Who wants to be respectable! I'd die of boredom, and so would you. After all, that's why you cleared out in the first place, isn't it? Your beloved Kintalloch and your priceless family simply bored you to death.'

'That was years ago. I've learned a lot since then.'

'Then why did you do a bunk the second time? Gave them the slip, didn't you? Or did they throw you out? You've never really told me what happened, have you?'

Angus was silent. There were moments when he still wanted to confide the unhappy business to her, knowing that she was capable of understanding and tenderness. But she seemed to be permanently in a bad temper these days. Perhaps after she's had the child, he thought. That might soften her a bit. He realized they had got into a vicious circle. His refusal to speak about why he had left Kintalloch infuriated her, which made it all the more impossible for him to give an explanation. There had been moments in the past when he had felt such rage against Nancy that he had been afraid he would murder her. Perhaps the temptation would come to him again if she started to vilify Meg. Besides, for the child's sake, he must try to keep things on an even keel.

'I left', he said, 'because I felt I couldn't fit in. But I was *not* bored. I was *not* suffering from a surfeit of respectability.'

'Well, I am,' she retorted, '*your* respectability.' Then, in a quieter tone she added:

'I think it's going to kill me.'

'What is?'

'This whole thing. Having the child, and being a mother and . . . everything.'

Suddenly it struck him that she was afraid. He got up and stood behind her chair, laying his hands on her shoulders.

'What is it, Nancy? What are you afraid of?'

'I didn't say I was afraid.' She still sounded defensive.

'You said you thought it was going to kill you. You're not afraid of dying in childbed, are you? That's a pretty old-fashioned sort of a concept.'

She shook her head:

'No, not that.'

'Then what?' He was speaking gently now, and Nancy responded by answering simply and quietly.

'I'm afraid I won't make a good mother,' she said.

'Because you don't want the child? It'll be different when it's here. You'll see.'

'But I don't see how having a baby to look after will make me more patient or methodical or better at coping with the housework. And there will obviously be so much more of that.'

'We'll manage,' he said, gently stroking her shoulders. 'We'll manage.'

Nancy said nothing. But after a moment she put her hands up and took hold of his, and held them for a long time, silent and comforted.

23

Meg had taken to spending a lot of her time upstairs again, standing in the hall.

Not out of misery as before; still less because of the connexion the place had with her meetings with Angus. This time the attraction of the hall, with its big windows, was the good view it gave of the drive. A few days before the child's birth was due Meg began to station herself there as often as possible, in the hope of catching the first glimpse of the telegraph boy. As it turned out, he arrived when they were all at a meal, so the news was nobody's private property. But as she waited day after day – for the child was late in arriving – she reflected with astonishment that little more than a year ago she had stood there, filled at first with only her own misery, and then with her longing for Angus to come with his comforting presence.

And now as she waited for news of his child with as much eagerness as if it were her own, it occurred to her that the whole episode with Angus would never have taken place if it hadn't been for her frustrated motherhood. First the loss of her own babies, then Gavin's refusal to consider adopting a child; that was what had done it. She felt sure Angus must have been thinking as much of her as of the rest of the family when he had offered the child to them. It was his way of making it up to her for leaving her behind.

And he must know that I shall love it as if it were my own, she thought. And it *will* be my own. In time this child will come here, and I shall be a mother to it, and the emptiness will leave my life at last.

It was Tom who received the telegram, and his hands were trembling so much that he couldn't open it.

'Give it to me,' said Bessie, serene in spite of the general excitement.

'Boy,' she read out triumphantly, 'all well.'

Angus had pondered a little over the wording of the telegram. The usual 'Both well' had seemed inappropriate, as Nancy didn't officially exist for the family.

The news provoked a scene of overt rejoicing such as seldom had been seen in this reticent family. They all leapt to their feet and rushed about, embracing each other. Then, as if nothing but violent action could express the exuberance of his feelings, Tom seized Meg and began dancing round the room with her. Gavin and his mother followed suit, and they all waltzed about for a while till Bessie recovered her normal sense of what was fitting, and ordered her husband to sit down at once.

'You're supposed to be taking it easy,' she chided, 'that's no way to treat your poor heart.'

Tom sat down, laughing and gasping.

'All right, all right,' he said, 'we can leave the dancing to the young folk. Go on, you two.'

But Gavin and Meg shook their heads, concerned about Tom's breathlessness.

The next few years were filled with a mixture of hope and exasperation for the Lindsay family. Secretly they had all hoped Nancy would turn out to be such a disastrous mother that the child would have to be sent to Kintalloch right away.

But Nancy seemed to be a good, if erratic, mother.

And, in spite of her spells of depression and not coping, she was evidently fond of the child. There was no question of rushing to take it away from her against her will.

Angus had wanted to call the child Thomas, after his own father. But Tom, though gratified at this, wanted his grandson to be named after his own father, Andrew. In the end this stalemate resulted in the child being christened Louis, a name both Scottish and French.

Meg, with her fondness for all things French, was particularly pleased. She had pondered much over what names to give her own children, and none of the possibilities she had considered before had pleased her as much as Louis.

24

'Well, Donald, here I am,' said Matilda as she sat down beside the bed. 'I've lots to tell you this morning, and I've brought a book to read to you from. Yes, I know that sentence ends with a preposition, but even Homer nods. Anyway, it's a volume of Emerson's essays.'

As she spoke she was taking the book out of her capacious bag, and looking for the page.

'Let's see. I think it was page ninety-seven. Yes, here it is.'

She settled down, holding the book in one hand. With the other she grasped Donald's hand as she always did when reading to him, hoping the contact might act as some sort of channel for the message that his hearing seemed unable to take in. But this time she let go of his hand at once and drew back, startled. The hand was as cold as marble. She touched him again and found that it was rigid.

Rigor mortis, she thought. He must have been dead a long time. And nobody seems to know. Matilda called a nurse and told her.

'Oh, no, Miss Hamilton. It can't be *rigor mortis.* That takes hours to set in. If he's dead it must have happened very recently.'

Together they went back to Donald's bedside.

'Oh, my God!' exclaimed the nurse as soon as she touched the frozen hand. 'I'd better go and tell Sister.'

There was a quiet commotion in the ward after that. It seemed that Donald's death had been as inopportune as his stroke. This time the event didn't occur at the wrong place, but at the wrong time. Because he was such an utterly undemanding patient, it appeared that the nurses did not always give him the usual amount of attention. As Sister explained, it was difficult to find time to go to a patient who was not asking for help, when so many others were. So it had come about that Donald had died quietly during the night, and no-one had found out.

Matilda was too shocked to say much. Besides, it was not for her to make a fuss. The hospital had always made it clear she was only there on sufferance, that she had no claims on them or their patient.

She limited herself to asking quietly, just before leaving:

'What are you going to tell Mrs Crombie? About the time of death, I mean. If you tell her the truth she will want to know why she has not been notified till half-way through the morning. You can hardly expect the doctor to put a false time on the death certificate. What are you going to do?'

Sister just stood there, looking perplexed and deflated. Then she rallied:

'The first thing I'm going to do is get hold of the night staff, and then the early morning staff. By the time I've finished with them . . . '

Matilda was left alone at the bedside. She took a last look at Donald. He looked exactly the same as he had for the last four years.

By the time Ellen arrived, Sister had worked out a plausible story:

Mr Crombie had died during the night, but the nurse on duty had forgotten to make sure that the information was passed on to Mrs Crombie. It had been a particularly busy night in the ward, and it wasn't till mid morning that they realized she hadn't been told.

Assuming Donald had not died unattended, and that the only thing wrong was their failure to notify her right away, Ellen felt she had no grounds for making an issue of the matter. Even if she had known earlier, there was nothing she could have done. She merely asked whether he had died peacefully.

'Yes, Mrs Crombie,' replied Sister, allowing probability to take the place of certainty, 'just slipped quietly away.'

* * *

After the funeral Ellen decided that there was no need for her to stay on in Edinburgh any longer. She wanted to go back to Kintalloch, but not to live in the house beside the others. Her mother had spent her last years living quietly in the lodge, and she felt she wanted to do the same. She could get on with her writing there, she would be near Meg, and when her long-awaited grand-nephew eventually came from France she would be able to share in the joy of his presence.

The others were all pleased with the plan. They were glad to think that Ellen would be near them, in her beloved Kintalloch – but yet not too near, as might have been the case if she had wanted to move in with them. Ellen wasn't exactly good at fitting in with other people, as Bessie remarked to Tom. He did not dispute the fact.

Meg too was glad her mother wasn't proposing to move in with the household. After eleven years of marriage she had now won for herself a certain position as a sort of unofficial second-in-command on the domestic scene. At last she felt she was no longer being treated as a delightful but fragile plaything. She was afraid this hard-earned balance might be disturbed if her mother entered the household. Not that there was any danger of Ellen's taking an active part in the running of the house. That was unthinkable. But the mere fact of having her mother under the same roof would have shaken her own image of herself as a fully-fledged adult.

So, after more than thirty years, Ellen came back to the lodge where she had lived with her mother before her marriage. She remembered how small it had seemed at first, when they moved in from the big house. Now, after her years in the spacious Edinburgh house, once again it seemed very small. But this time she had it all to herself. There was room enough for her books and papers, and that was all she needed. She sold the house in

161

Edinburgh and practically everything in it without giving it a second thought.

Bessie shook her head over the transaction.

'Really, Meg,' she said, 'your mother is quite remarkable. I've never known anyone so indifferent to material things. She's a lesson to us all.' After a pause, she added:

'I suppose.'

Meg smiled. 'I see what you mean,' she said. For she realized that her mother, if lacking any interest in the material things of this world, was also lacking in the human warmth and spontaneity of lesser mortals.

I wonder where I fit in, she thought. I don't think I'm very materialistic. But then, I've always had plenty of everything, at least where the goods of this world are concerned. She came to the conclusion that she was rather like her mother in this respect, and wondered whether she had also inherited a share of her distance and apparent indifference. She felt sure people thought she was like that, because of her reserve. Then it struck her that perhaps in her mother's case it was also a question of reserve. She gave a great sigh. How little we know of each other, she thought. And of ourselves.

Within a few days of being back in the lodge Ellen felt more at home than ever she had in Edinburgh. She was often invited up for a meal with the others, and they frequently dropped in to see her. She and Meg took to having long rambles about the countryside, as Ellen had done as a child with Tom. But most of her time was spent alone in the little house, reading and writing, and thinking about her poems. Her poetic activities she mentioned to no-one. She still thought about trying to publish, sooner or later, but she also felt that her poetry was just getting past the juvenilia stage.

So she would wait till she had found a more certain voice.

There was no hurry.

After all, she wasn't trying to build a career for herself, was she?

25

Matilda had known she couldn't go to the funeral.

But she found out when it was to take place and where Donald was to be buried, and in the afternoon she went to the cemetery and stood beside the new grave. Then she went home and asked herself what she was going to do with her life. Since Donald's illness her afternoons and evenings had been empty. Now this emptiness swallowed up the whole day. There was nothing she had to do and nothing she wanted to do. But she had always thought of herself as a woman of character, and knew she must soon decide what to do with the rest of her life. First, however, there was nothing she could do but grieve.

And she was amazed at the extent of her sorrow.

For four years she had known that Donald might die at any minute. For four years she had had no sort of companionship from him. Why then did his death plunge her into such a black pit of sorrow? Suddenly the Donald she had known during their happy years together seemed to come back in startling reality. She was oppressed by memories of intolerable sweetness. The combination of his almost palpable presence and the knowledge that their separation was now finally, utterly irrevocable was more than she could bear. She sat for hours staring at his picture on her mantelpiece, while the tears flowed down her cheeks.

At last reaction set in. Matilda was sitting crying in front of his picture one afternoon when the words came into her head:

'If only he could see me now!' She came to the conclusion that Donald would be most disappointed in her. He had always admired her firmness and realistic approach to life. This was not what he would have expected of her, even if the tears were all on his account. No, she thought, I must pull myself together, I must decide what to do with my life. I'll take my time about it. I'm too emotional to make a rational decision just yet. I'll give myself a month. By that time I should have come up with something. I'm an intelligent woman of sixty-three, with a well trained mind and a small but regular income. There must be many things worth doing for a woman in my position. By the fifteenth of next month I'll have made a decision. Meanwhile I'll write down every possibility that comes into my head.

Two weeks later she had quite a list of possible pursuits written down – gardening, social work, learning about birds, writing her memoirs, philosophy, brushing up her Latin – but still she had come to no decision.

I've still got a couple of weeks, she thought. If I haven't decided by then, I'll write down all my options on pieces of paper and draw one out of a hat.

When the fifteenth came she knew that what she really wanted most was to write her memoirs. But this would not be feasible if she was going to be honest, and nothing short of absolute honesty would do. There was no way of glossing over, or missing out, the two unavowable episodes in her life; and yet she could not bring herself to implicate others in her not irreproachable past.

No, memoirs wouldn't do.

In the end she opted for taking up water-colours. She had always been good at drawing, and would have liked to take it further, but had never got round to it. This scheme had the advantage that it would put her in touch with other people, even if only for a couple of hours a week at evening classes. Her life had become very isolated over the past years and she realized she was in danger of becoming a recluse. To be a hermit for the love of God – or even for the dislike of man – was one thing. But to let oneself become one through sheer apathy was a pretty feeble thing to do. Matilda did not intend to be feeble. Besides, there was another aspect to the painting scheme that appealed to her. She had always envied painters, musicians, writers – people who gave something to the world.

We are given so much, she thought. Gifts from nature, gifts

created for us by the artists of the world – how wonderful to be able to give something back, however little. Well, she was now going to make her first small attempt at repayment. If no-one wanted what she had to offer, that was another matter. Even if she did not manage to give back any of the pleasure she had received, she would have tried.

I shall not hide my talent, if talent there be, she thought, taking pleasure in her use of the subjunctive.

26

'I thought your mother would have been here by now, Meg. Isn't it today she's supposed to come for lunch?'

Meg looked up. 'Yes, it's today. Is that the time? I'm surprised she's not here. Shall I run down to the lodge and see if she's forgotten?'

'Yes, I think you'd better. You know what her memory is like.'

Meg put on her coat and set off down the drive. There was a cold, autumnal feel to the air, and she would rather have stayed in. Perhaps it would be just as well if her mother didn't venture out. She had a bit of cold, and hadn't looked too well the last day or two.

When she got to the lodge she found her mother in bed, looking feverish.

'It's just that cold,' Ellen said, 'it suddenly seemed to get worse yesterday. I meant to be up in time for lunch, but I just fell asleep.'

Meg said she thought they'd better get the doctor.

'Oh, I don't want that young puppy they've got now. I wish Doc hadn't taken it into his head to retire.'

Meg smiled. 'Well, he is over eighty, you know. Most people have retired long before that.'

Ellen dug in her heels. 'If I can't have Doc I'll have no-one. All I need is a good sleep, anyway. Go back and have your lunch. I'm all right.'

Meg went back, not very convinced. In the afternoon she and Bessie went back to the lodge, and the two of them decided to override Ellen's protests and send for the doctor.

He came, examined his reluctant patient, and diagnosed pneumonia. He made it clear that he should have been sent for earlier.

'But we didn't know she was ill. She just said she had a cold a couple of days ago, that was all.'

The doctor nodded. 'Yes, that's how it usually starts.'

In spite of the treatment Ellen's state deteriorated. They were told they would have to wait for the crisis in a few days' time. After that they could hope for a fairly sudden improvement, if things went well. Nothing was said about the other alternative.

Meg moved into the little room her mother had as a girl, and they hired a night nurse to help her. Ellen seemed to spend most of the time sleeping, and there was little to do except sit beside her in case she needed anything. They weren't sure whether she recognized them or not. But then, it was always rather that way with Ellen anyway, as Bessie pointed out. You never quite knew to what extent she was with you.

Several days went by with no apparent change, except that the patient seemed to be getting weaker. Meg was asleep one night in the little bedroom when the night nurse came to waken her.

'I see a change in your mother,' she said, 'she seems quite lucid and she's asking for you.'

As she got up Meg asked, 'Does this mean she's improving?'

'Not necessarily,' replied the nurse. 'Sometimes . . . ' She made a vague gesture.

By this time Meg had her dressing gown on and she hurried into her mother's room.

For the first few months after moving to the lodge Ellen had felt her poetry was coming on quite nicely. And then she struck an arid patch, when nothing seemed to work. At first she didn't let this bother her. She'd had spells like this before. It was just a question of waiting a little and it would come all right. She waited and still nothing happened. The fountain seemed to have dried up. For months she struggled to find her voice again. Eventually she decided that what she needed was a complete change of direction. Her first phase had produced intense and sometimes tortured love poetry. After that she had changed the subject and form, and a new source of inspiration seemed to have opened up to her. But looking back she saw that, although the subject matter had changed, the spirit hadn't. The poems were still predominantly tormented and negative. She now felt that the time had come to affirm. But this was where the difficulty lay. The path that led to affirmation seemed blocked in some way. She came to the conclusion that she would not be able to move forward till she had found out what the obstruction was, and removed it.

Self-examination was something that came fairly easily to Ellen. She remembered that her last leap forward in the creative experience had come not only when she decided to change the form and subject matter of her poetry, but also after the poems had helped her to realize that she had lived her life falsely, seeing herself as an innocent victim because she had been accused of a sin that she hadn't committed, but would have if she'd been given the chance. Dimly she felt that this block – this obstruction that was keeping her from writing – might be something of the same nature, something she had to do, or something she had to recognize within herself.

She tried writing again, but all her attempts straggled into nothingness.

> There is no rightness like the rightness of round flowers.
> Round centre, petals radiating,
> Circle within concentric circle . . .

Nothing more came, and she wasn't all that pleased with these three lines anyway. The idea was all right; it was a subject she felt happy about. Round flowers had recently become her favourites. She now found herself almost repelled by the complications of an orchid or an aquilegia. They seemed poor, confused creatures beside the simple beauty of the daisy, or the opulent roundness of the rose. That was the poem she wanted to write, but she just couldn't write it.

168

Perhaps when she had got rid of this beastly cold . . . But deep down she felt there was something more than a cold she had to get rid of. After the cold got worse, and she took to her bed, her preoccupation with this obstruction that had got between her and her poetry became almost an obsession. During the hours of semi-sleep that followed she became aware of a tall figure flitting about on the edges of her consciousness and she knew that there was some unresolved business between this woman and herself.

And then the thread came.

During her few childhood illnesses, when the fever was high, she was often tormented by the sight of a thread being drawn across her field of vision, which was limited to about ten or twelve inches. The thread was being drawn horizontally across, always from right to left, and its appearance varied enormously. When the thread was thin and taut, moving along steadily, all was well. With it came a great sense of peace. But then the thread would start to waver, its movement became less steady, and this change was always associated with a great sense of foreboding. Soon the thread thickened, sometimes even reaching a thickness of a quarter of an inch, and the movement became increasingly unsteady. This change always brought with it a sensation of intense distress. Sometimes things were even worse, and the thickness of the thread became uneven, like a piece of slubbed cotton. When this happened her distress became unbearable, and she would cry out in her fever. She had often remembered this symptom, or dream, or whatever it was, but had not experienced it for about fifty years. And now it was back, as threatening and unbearable as before. Sometimes, as the thread regained its thin, taut state and her distress diminished, she caught glimpses of the tall figure in the wings of her consciousness.

Now the thread was running steadily: thin, fine, taut; bringing with it that sense of great peace. It ran on and on, till it ran itself out of her field of vision. And then she saw the figure clearly. It was Matilda Hamilton, and suddenly she knew what her business with her was. It's the same sort of thing again, she thought. I've been indulging in unjustified resentment. A case of false pretences again. For she realized – and why had she not seen this before? she wondered – that this woman had not stolen her husband from her. She had lost her husband many years before, when something, and she still didn't know what, had brought about the sudden estrangement that had kept them apart from then on. Perhaps, she thought, perhaps this is the obstruction that's keeping me from being able to write. If I put this right, perhaps the poetry will come again. Perhaps I shall be whole again.

'Meg!' she called out. 'Meg! I want to speak to my daughter,' she told the nurse.

Meg went into the room and sat down on the bed. She took her mother's hand in hers and said, 'Yes, Mother?'

There was a long pause, as if Ellen were trying to summon up enough strength to speak again. Then she whispered:

'Miss Hamilton.'

'Do you want to see Miss Hamilton?' Meg was surprised. They hadn't mentioned the governess's name in years.

Ellen shook her head. 'No, you,' she whispered.

'You want me to see Miss Hamilton? What about?'

Ellen's eyes had closed again, and Meg wondered whether she had fallen asleep. After a few minutes Ellen spoke again, so faintly that Meg was only able to make out two words:

'Olive branch.' Then her mother's eyes closed and there was silence.

Meg went to get the nurse. She didn't know whether her mother was alive or dead.

Ellen sank back into her semi-conscious state after that. The tall figure had disappeared. The thread was there again. But now it was a source of endless joy. For what seemed to be hours she watched it move along, from right to left: thin, fine, taut.

Suddenly it snapped.

170

27

A few days after the funeral, Meg decided she had better carry out what seemed to be her mother's last wishes, and go and see Miss Hamilton.

She had spent the last hours of her mother's life sitting by the bedside, puzzling over the meaning of those last words. It appeared that her mother wanted her to go to Miss Hamilton as an olive branch, but in connexion with what she couldn't imagine. Presumably they had had some sort of a quarrel that she had heard nothing about. Perhaps that would explain why Miss Hamilton had disappeared from their horizon and why her mother never mentioned her. She had no idea what the subject of their disagreement could have been, or when it might have taken place. She remembered that her mother had not shown any constraint in the matter of the letter in which Miss Hamilton had declined the invitation to the wedding. In fact, she remembered that Ellen had told her to keep the letter, which she evidently viewed with approval.

There had obviously been no ill-feeling then.

As far as she knew there had been no further contact between the two women. It was very puzzling and rather disturbing. Being an olive branch must inevitably have some difficulties attached to the position. What sort of a reception would Miss Hamilton give her? Would she explain what the problem had been? And if so, on whose side should she be? Time and again she was on the point of telling Gavin, and asking his advice. But always she was held back by the certainty that there must be something discreditable about the whole thing, otherwise what need was there of an olive branch? Meg was very pacific by nature, and always felt that any quarrel was a shameful thing for both parties. If at all possible, she felt it was her duty to try and protect her mother's memory from such a stain.

So she set off for Edinburgh by herself one day, saying she had business with the lawyer about her mother's estate. This was the truth, though not the whole truth: a situation Meg felt tolerably comfortable in, though she disliked any form of subterfuge.

She hoped none of her forebodings would turn out to be justified, and that she would be able to tell all the family what the situation was without having to implicate her mother in anything unpleasant or discreditable.

Meg remembered where Miss Hamilton lived. After all, how could she forget that memorable afternoon, with the two-tram journey in her mother's company, her *tête-à-tête* with Miss Hamilton, and then her father's arrival and the delightful, lively conversation that followed? The trouble was, of course, that after so many years Miss Hamilton might well have moved house. In that case she would have to get what information she could from the neighbours. As she wasn't sure of the number she told the taxi driver to put her down at the end of the street, and started walking. She knew it was about half-way along, on the right, and hoped she would recognize the house, or at least the garden. She wasn't used to tackling this sort of problem on her own, and was feeling quite shaky by the time she got to the house. Seeing the name 'Hamilton' on a small brass plate, she knew this must be it.

Trembling like a leaf at the thought of the interview ahead of her, Meg tried to steady herself by taking a few deep breaths. Then she pressed the doorbell and waited.

Matilda Hamilton was at that moment standing in her sitting room, looking critically at the painting she was working on. The art lessons had not been an unqualified success. Her ideas about the use of the medium did not appear to coincide with those of the teacher.

'Ye-es, ye-es,' he would say, looking at her colourful efforts. 'I see you've certainly got something to say, but that's really not the way to use water-colours, you know. Don't you think your colours are perhaps a bit strident? I mean, suppose you washed that bit down a little, just to make it more delicate? After all, delicacy is the chief characteristic of water-colour.'

Matilda didn't see why it should be. He tried to persuade her to try painting in oils. She refused. Oils were too expensive for her. Then he suggested pen and ink, or charcoal. Plenty of contrast there, you know. But Matilda wanted her contrast in colour. They stuck it out for the term, annoying and putting up with each other, and then Matilda decided she would just have to go on by herself. Next year, perhaps, she would try again with another teacher, if she could find one that was prepared to consider what *could* be done rather than what *should* be done with water-colours.

When she opened the front door she was still thinking of her painting. For a few seconds the two women stared at each other in silence. Matilda spoke first, but all she could say was:

'Oh, Meg!' Then she stood aside for Meg to enter. 'Come in, my dear.'

In the hall they stood and looked at each other again for a moment.

'I heard about your mother, Meg. I'm so sorry.'

Meg felt she ought to say that it was her mother who had sent her, but knew she would burst into tears if she said anything at all.

Seeing her distress, Matilda ushered her into the sitting room and asked her to sit down. As Meg advanced to one of the two armchairs by the fire, her eyes fell on the mantelpiece. On it was a photograph of her father. She gave a little exclamation and turned to look at Matilda with shock and reproach written all over her features.

At last she found her voice. 'So it was you,' she said in little more than a whisper.

'You didn't know?'

Meg shook her head. She looked so pale and distraught that Matilda was quite alarmed.

'Sit down, Meg,' she said, 'you've had a shock. And just after the loss of your mother, too. Please, sit down while I make a cup of tea. Then we can talk.'

Meg was glad of a respite. Perhaps she would be able to get her thoughts and emotions in order with a few minutes on her own.

In the kitchen Matilda's first reaction was regret that the photograph had been there. Without it Meg would have been spared this shock. On the other hand, she reflected, since she has come, for whatever reason, we must talk, and that means she has to know the truth. For me this way was certainly easier than having to put it into words. But poor Meg!

The first few minutes after her return to the sitting room were spent dealing with the business of serving tea. Matilda's thoughts were occupied with the recollection of the last cup of tea she had served Donald. She was now sitting in the chair she had found him slumped in after his stroke, while Meg sat in the chair opposite.

Meg's thoughts were evidently running along similar lines, for she said:

'So this is where my father was taken ill?'

'Yes, he was sitting in this armchair, where I am now. But tell me, Meg, what brought you?'

'My mother sent me.'

'Your mother?'

'Yes. Her very last words. She asked me to come to you, and then I was able to make out nothing else, except for the words *olive branch*. But I couldn't imagine what it was all about. Now I know.' And her eyes turned again to the photograph of her father.

'And you knew nothing?'

'I knew what had happened, but not where. Mother knew, and admitted as much, but she said the less I knew about it the better.

And I accepted that. We're not a very communicative family. I felt her need for silence on the matter was greater than my need for the facts. And I couldn't go behind her back and try to find out from anyone else.'

Matilda looked at Meg with a sad and gentle expression. 'That's my Meg,' she said with a little smile. 'Just what I would have expected of you. And now of course you can see why your mother was so particularly anxious to protect you from knowing . . . who was involved. And now she . . . Oh, I wish I knew what has been going on in her mind all these years, and what brought her to wish for a reconciliation. For I assume that's what she meant. Don't you?'

Meg admitted that she could find no other interpretation. 'And now that I do know, will you please tell me the whole story?' She felt utterly baffled by the problem of what she ought to be feeling for her old governess. Her conflicting loyalties were being torn violently in different directions. Perhaps things would be a bit clearer if she knew the whole story.

Matilda had no problems with conflicting loyalties. Her whole effort now was directed towards trying to reconcile Meg to what had happened:

'Yes, I'll tell you everything, everything that could possibly be relevant. But first of all, there's one thing I want to make absolutely clear. Your father was a good man, Meg, a very good man. There was nothing light or irresponsible about him or about our relationship, even though the facts may seem to prove the contrary. I'm not saying he never did anything wrong. We all do. But the good in him was infinitely greater than the bad, so we cannot pass judgement on him.'

She started at the beginning, at the tea party Meg so well remembered, with its sequel in the form of Donald's first, frustrated advances. She hesitated about telling of her own refusal of these advances on the grounds of the incompatibility of the two roles she was being asked to assume at the same time. Meg might take it as an attempt at self-justification. But she had promised to tell the whole truth; and besides, the fact that Donald had accepted her decision to choose the daughter rather than the father, and not approached her again till her connexion with the family had been severed, was at least something to be said in his favour.

After a pause Matilda continued:

'There's one other thing I must tell you, though it's difficult because it might sound like an attempt to justify myself. It is only because it goes a long way towards justifying your father that I feel I must tell it. It was not I who destroyed your parents' marriage. They had been deeply estranged for many years before I met them. I know they kept up the appearance of a harmoniously married couple; but for years they had lived lives apart in everything but appearance. You may even remember something of this, for your father told me that at the time of the rupture you were upset.'

Meg looked up, startled. 'Would this be when I was about five?'

'Yes. So you remember?'

'Yes. I didn't know what was wrong, but I remember the aura of unhappiness that engulfed us all. And from then on we saw far less of my father in the house. Did he tell you what was wrong?'

'To a certain extent. It seems he heard certain rumours about something in your mother's past. He was never able to get over this. He felt it had destroyed his marriage.'

'Rumours about what? Did he say?'

Matilda permitted herself a lie on this occasion. It seemed to her that the truth was far more hurtful than anything Meg could possibly suppose. 'No. And anyway, what the rumours were was relatively unimportant. What mattered was whether they were truthful or not. It seems that, because of the special circumstances of the case, there was no way your father could get at the true facts.'

'But did he not ask my mother?'

'Apparently not. Your mother was a very silent, reserved person, not easy to approach. And besides, if he could have no corroboration from outside . . . His profession had taught him how we all lie in our own defence.'

Meg suddenly remembered her subterfuges to meet Angus in private. She felt herself blushing painfully.

'I don't know whether there would be any truth in the rumours about your mother,' went on Matilda. 'From what I know of her, I think it most unlikely. It's a great pity that your father took the attitude he did. But it would be hypocritical of me to pretend that I regretted this. Without this estrangement between your parents I should have missed the most important and happiest relationship of my life. We are all rather patchy creatures, Meg. I don't want you to think ill of either of your parents. They were both good, sincere people, and they both had remarkable qualities.'

They then spoke about what could have prompted Ellen's desire to be reconciled with Matilda. Perhaps just an awareness of approaching death, suggested Meg. But she had to admit she had no idea what was going on in her mother's mind – then, or at any time.

'I wish we weren't such a secretive family,' she sighed. 'I suppose I'm just as bad.'

She was too overwhelmed by all she had learned that day to know how she ought to feel towards any of the protagonists in the story that had been unfolded to her. Matilda realized this, and did not try to prolong the interview. But she did ask Meg to come and see her again.

'I think all the barriers that divided us have crumbled now,' she said. 'It has been a great grief to me, to be separated from you all these years.'

Meg suddenly remembered the valedictory nature of the letter declining the invitation to her wedding. She looked up and managed a wan smile. 'Yes, I'll come again when things have settled down.' By 'things' she realized she meant her own emotions as much as the external circumstances of her life.

In the train she wondered how much she ought to tell the others. Then she thought what a lot of this sad tangle could have been avoided, given a little more openness all round. So she would tell them all, right down to the last detail. It was time they stopped being such a secretive family. Who could tell how much more damage might be wreaked if they all carried on in this way! And how surprised they would be, would they not, when they heard of Miss Hamilton's part in the affair!

28

The surprise was in fact Meg's – when she discovered that they had known all along that Matilda Hamilton was the other woman. It took her a while to understand the chagrin she felt over this. Then she realized it was not simply because her dramatic revelation had fallen flat. It was because this was another example of the way they treated her, like a child who has to be protected all the time.

True to her new resolution she pointed this out to Gavin, rather pleased with herself for having the courage to do so. But instead of apologizing Gavin explained that at the time not only had she been upset by her father's sudden and terrible illness, but she herself had been in a very fragile state after the loss of the baby. It would have been unnecessarily cruel to give her the full facts when the knowledge of Miss Hamilton's part in the affair would have been bound to add enormously to her suffering.

'That's true,' she admitted. 'I hadn't thought of that. But you might have told me afterwards.'

'What would have been the point? And anyway, it was a subject we never spoke about. Some things are better forgotten.'

'Yes. But will you promise not to hide things from me in future? I'm nearly thirty-one years old, and quite grown up.' And to prove it she jumped up and sat on his lap.

It was some weeks before Meg was able to bring herself to go through her mother's papers. It seemed like an act of sheer voyeurism. She was still uncertain what to do when she opened the big desk in Ellen's bedroom. The mere fact that Ellen had always kept all her papers in her bedroom seemed to underline her desire for total privacy.

There were several bundles of papers put tidily away, with rubber bands to keep them together. Then Meg found some loose sheets of paper, with writing on them. She was gathering these together, still not sure she ought to read any of them, when she noticed one with just a single line of writing:

There is no rightness like the rightness of round flowers.

That's an odd thing to write, Meg thought. She picked up one of the neat bundles of papers, and saw a label on it:

'For Publication?'

Suddenly it struck her that these papers were not, ultimately, meant to be private. She felt she had to read them and see what could be done to get them published.

She read through the whole bundle labelled 'For Publication?' and was startled by the bleakness and even despair that they expressed. One in particular, entitled 'Sinking', suggested a frightening pessimism.

Long ago there was water too
but it was different –
dark torrents that poured down the mountainside
and bore me with them, struggling and appalled
half-drowned and desperate.
But when the storm had passed
it left me lying in the sun, rejoicing
on some familiar shore.
Then there was much more land than water
and the land was bright and the storms few.
Now the waters have grown vast and still and secret.
One black and stagnant swamp
covers the land I loved and trusted in.
The trees and fields and valleys are submerged
and all the roads are gone.
Now only shadowy islands here and there,
muddy and desolate.
These were my mountain tops.
Slowly they crumble beneath me.
I sink into the silent black waters

and strike out yet again in search of the mainland
and find only these
impermanent islands.
Perhaps now
there is no mainland.

Meg took some consolation from the fact that the loose sheets, which were presumably the ones Ellen was working on at her death, seemed to have lost all trace of this terrible pessimism.

When she came to the bundle of love poems she assumed that they were written about her father retrospectively, for many were dated within the last few years. She was startled, not to say shocked, by the carnal quality of many of these poems. Her mother had always seemed so cool and detached from the physical world, it seemed incongruous that she should be capable of writing such intensely physical love poetry. It struck her that, if her mother had loved her husband in this way, it must have been peculiarly cruel for her to have to live most of her married life estranged from him.

Then she came across a poem, written only a few years ago, with the title 'Fifth January, 1877'.

Mother's birthday, thought Meg. It must have been her seventh birthday.

She started reading it expectantly, hoping to find some childhood recollection, and at the same time wondering why it was included among the love poems.

We have been torn asunder, you and I
my love, my lover, you
who shared my mother's womb with me, say why
my love, my lover, why
must we conform to this fierce deity
that tears apart what flesh has joined together?

It's not true, Meg thought angrily. It *can't* be true. And

181

yet . . . she wrote it herself, it's *her* writing. Feeling sick with shock and misery, Meg read on.

The rest of the poem was equally explicit.

By the end of the afternoon she felt totally incapable of tackling the problem of what to do about the poems, or even what to believe about them. Was it possible that her mother and Uncle Tom had had an incestuous relationship? Was this the subject of the rumours that had separated her parents? And who, of all the family, knew about this?

She was torn between a desperate desire to know more, and a conviction that she should keep the dark truth to herself. Uncle Tom, of course, would be the one person who could tell her. But how could she approach him on such a matter? Besides, he wasn't at all well at the moment. Then it occurred to her that his indisposition had started just after her mother's death, and she wondered whether this pointed to a closer bond than she had realized.

She got back to the house in a state of collapse. Bessie took one look at her and sent her off to bed.

'You've been overdoing it, Meg,' she said. 'You've spent all afternoon on those papers of your mother's. It's sad work, and exhausting. I know it has to be done, but not all at once.'

Bessie put her arm round Meg's waist to help her up the stairs. Suddenly Meg stopped and whispered, 'Oh, I can't bear it, I can't bear it.' Then she burst into tears and buried her face on Bessie's shoulder. They stood there, half-way up the stairs, for some time, till Bessie coaxed her into making the final effort to reach the bedroom. There Meg let herself be put to bed like a sick child. Almost petulantly she refused to let them send for the doctor; then said yes, she would like him to come, but it must be Doc.

'I know he's retired,' she said, 'but surely he'll come for me?'

Bessie assured her that she would send for her father right away.

182

It had suddenly occurred to Meg that Doc was the very person she needed to see. Having known the family since her mother was a child, he was sure to have heard the rumours, and perhaps he even knew the truth. Apart from Uncle Tom, whom she felt she could not possibly approach on the subject, no-one else could help her as much.

Meg knew that nothing anybody said could disprove the evidence of Ellen's own words, but she still longed for some assurance that could at least comfort her and restore her image of her mother.

Briefly she told Doc about the poems, and showed him the one her mother had written about her seventh birthday, as well as some other love poems.

When he had read them he gave them back to Meg, saying:

'Poor thing, poor thing. She must have suffered greatly.'

'But Doc, is it true? It must be true, she wouldn't invent such a situation, would she?'

'No, she wouldn't invent it.'

'And the rumours, they must have been about that. Did you hear the rumours?'

'Most people heard them.'

'And they were true?'

'Look, Meg, there are degrees of truth. I think there's no doubt that your mother and her brother were passionately attached to each other as children. If I remember rightly, the poem about her birthday refers to a time when their parents decided that, for their own sakes, they should not sleep together any longer. People were talking already – remember, this was in eighteen seventy-seven, in the full flood of Victorian morality – and people, unfortunately, continued to talk for many, many years after. My guess is that, as they grew older, your mother's attachment stayed as it was, whereas her brother, while still fond of her, didn't let his love for her develop into anything unhealthy.'

'So you don't think there ever was an incestuous relation-ship?'

'Probably not.'

'But that poem, and all the love poems – which I see now must have been about Uncle Tom, and not, as I thought at first, about my father. You can't get away from what those poems reveal.'

'This is what I meant about different degrees of truth. There's factual truth – something happens or it doesn't, one or the other. Then there's emotional truth. I'm prepared to believe your mother may have wanted that sort of relationship with her brother. That doesn't mean it ever really existed. But for a sensitive, thoughtful woman like your mother that was enough to make it one of the facts to be reckoned with in her life. Not the action, simply the desire.

'And then there's artistic truth. A poem may make any claims or any assumptions it likes. It has its own truth, which may have nothing to do with what actually happened. From the point of view of the poem, does it matter whether Wordsworth actually saw his solitary reaper? Or whether he just imagined her?'

Meg reflected for a while, then said:

'But I can't bear to think that my mother was capable of even wanting such a wicked thing.'

'Do you know, Meg, I'm two generations older than you are! Yet anyone might think it was the other way round, from the way we look at things. You've led an unusually sheltered life, and have very little idea of what things are really like in the ordinary everyday world. My profession has brought me into contact with all sorts of human problems. *Even if* you assume your mother wanted an incestuous relationship with her brother, think of it as her misfortune, nothing more. A mistake on the part of nature. We all suffer from that, one way or another. Old Mother Nature is wonderful, but she's never yet made a perfect man or woman, not since the world began. Anyway,' he added thoughtfully, 'I think your mother was sort of pushed into an extreme position by those rumours. What might have died a natural death was kept alive in this way. And you Lindsays, always so shut in and turned in upon yourselves! If your mother had gone to boarding school like Tom, she might have outgrown the whole thing, like Tom. And there's another thing. If I hadn't been certain there was no truth in the rumours, I wouldn't have let your uncle marry my daughter, would I?'

'Well, I'm glad you did.'

'Yes, I think it's been a very successful marriage. Provided you with a pretty good husband, eh?'

After this conversation Meg began to recover her emotional balance. She now felt she had no further need to discuss the matter with anyone. And what Doc had said about her Victorian attitude to life and the Lindsay tendency to involution strengthened her resolve to be more open, less prone to the family secretiveness. This one subject, however, was to be the exception. This was her mother's secret, not hers.

The problem that remained was whether she should try to publish certain poems. After all, her mother had not left any clear indication. Simply the query:

'For Publication?'

29

Meg had no idea how to set about finding a publisher, and rather wished she could persuade herself there was no need to try. Then she remembered her promise to visit Miss Hamilton again. Of all the people she knew, her old governess was surely the best qualified to evaluate the poems, and to advise on publication.

Meg decided that next time she went to see Matilda Hamilton she would take the poems with her. Not the love poems, of course. These she felt she really ought to destroy. They were surely too private, even without the suspicion of incest. She regretted that this left only the poems of utter despair. The few lines on the sheets of work in progress were more positive, but there was nothing like a complete poem among them; just those few tantalising lines. Meg thought this a pity, because these fragments seemed to her more like what poetry ought to be — something that helped to lift you up, rather than knock you down at every turn. She had still to learn the value of catharsis.

While thinking about the poems she remembered a little trick of her mother's that had puzzled her during the past few years. Often when they were sitting together in silence, Ellen would move her fingers in an odd way, tapping gently against her thigh, always starting with her little finger, then moving each one in turn, then starting again at the little finger. Meg had assumed this was just some nervous habit Ellen had got into, a way of dealing with the stress of her husband's illness and death. Now she realized her mother had probably been counting syllables. During those long silences she must have been mentally writing her poems. Meg felt a little shiver go down her spine as she thought of the content of so many of them. Either carnal and forbidden love, or else despair. Then she thought of Doc's words:

'Poor thing, poor thing, she must have suffered greatly.'

* * *

Matilda was impressed by the selection of Ellen's poetry Meg presented to her, and agreed to try to get them published. After some months she had to report back to Meg that her efforts had not been successful. The poems had been admired but rejected by all the publishers she approached.

'There was one,' she admitted, 'who seemed quite reluctant to decline, but did so on the ground that the collection is too slight. Not enough poems, he said, to make even the slimmest of volumes.'

This news filled Meg with guilt and doubt, and she confessed there had been others which she had burnt, as being of too personal a nature. 'They were in a separate bundle – not the one marked: 'For Publication?' I wonder whether I did the right thing, after all, in burning them.'

'I'm sure you did. We couldn't possibly offer for publication any poem she had excluded from the chosen group.'

Matilda suspected that Ellen might not really have minded the idea of having the more personal ones published posthumously, but refrained from mentioning this to Meg. If the poems were destroyed there was nothing to be done about it. No need to upset poor Meg further.

Meg had walked over to the table at the window where Matilda did her drawing and painting. There was an almost finished work in progress, and Meg was struck by the subject.

'Goodness!' she exclaimed, 'this reminds me of one of my mother's poems, the one about sinking, with the bit about the impermanent islands.'

'Does it really? I'm so glad. That's precisely what I was thinking of when I started on it.'

Matilda had stuck to her resolution about going on with her water-colours in her own way. This particular painting was done in very strong, sombre colours, and depicted a raging sea with a few islands separated by swirling waters. One of the islands appeared to be crumbling away.

'In fact,' continued Matilda, 'that's what I meant to call this one – Impermanent Islands. As you see, your mother's poetry has had a profound effect on me. I'm thinking of doing a whole series of paintings on the subject.'

There was a brief pause, and then both women looked at each other, surprised and hopeful.

'Do you think we could perhaps combine the two?' asked Meg.

'Possibly. If you think my work is good enough to stand beside your mother's.'

'I'm sure it is. Oh, Miss Hamilton, it would be wonderful if your work and hers could appear together in the book!'

Matilda had private reservations about her own standard, but she agreed to go back to the more encouraging publisher and suggest the inclusion of her own paintings in the volume. She remembered that one of her reasons for taking up water-colours was the desire to offer something to the world, however modest. So perhaps this was her chance. She also liked the idea of a book combining work by the two women Donald had loved. Sometimes she wondered what Ellen would have thought of it; but when she voiced this doubt to Meg the reply was:

'Don't forget my mother's last wish. That I should come and see you. As her "olive branch".'

Matilda's illustrations, according to the publisher, were just what was required to make the book viable. Both Meg and Matilda were looking forward to receiving their first finished copies, when a telegram from Paris arrived at Kintalloch:

PLEASE COME FOR LOUIS STOP URGENT STOP ANGUS.

30

The first years of Louis's life were much less stressful than either of his parents expected. Nancy took a liking to her baby from the start, and showed herself to be a devoted, if rather haphazard, mother. The child's helplessness evoked all her tenderness, and as Louis grew older she enjoyed playing with him, making up little games, and generally having fun on a level suited to toddlers. Angus was relieved, but realized he would have to keep constant watch; for Nancy still suffered from her black moods, and sometimes would virtually ignore the child for days on end. Then the mood would lift, and she would indulge Louis in all sorts of illicit pleasures.

Neither health nor discipline counted for much when it came to amusing the child. There were frequent arguments about how to bring him up, but on the whole Angus was relieved to find things going far better than expected. He had to be ready to take over at any moment, when Nancy's spirits flagged, and, for the child's sake, he had to master his own tendency to erratic living. He felt it was rather unfair that Louis evidently adored his mother, and showed distinctly less eagerness to be with his father, but he accepted it as philosophically as he could. After all, he could at least have the satisfaction of knowing that, even if it was Nancy who provided the fun and the frills, he was taking care of the essentials.

Sometimes, when he saw the bond between Louis and his mother, he worried about his promise to hand the child over to Kintalloch as soon as he was old enough. Perhaps he had been rash in making the suggestion. He realized now that he had been more concerned with trying to make up for his defection from the family circle than with the happiness of either the child or Nancy. But how could anyone have guessed that so reluctant a mother-to-be would turn into such a happy, affectionate mother?

It wasn't till Louis was nearly three that Nancy's spells of gloom began to come more frequently and to last longer. Angus was getting used to coming home and finding Nancy sitting hunched up in a chair, with nothing done, and Louis wandering about the flat, whining, dirty and hungry.

One day, soon after one of these bouts of gloom had started, he was surprised to come home and find her looking bright and lively, getting a meal ready in the kitchen. His relief, however, soon turned to near despair, when he caught the smell of alcohol on her breath.

He remonstrated.

Nancy laughed and assured him it was nothing. Just a tiny drop because she was feeling so low. 'You can see what a good idea it was, I'm feeling fine now. I've done the shopping, I've even made the bed, and I'll have a lovely meal ready for you in a little while. Louis likes his mummy to be happy. Don't you, my darling?'

The child, of course, agreed wholeheartedly. A happy mummy provided all sorts of dainties, and an unhappy one left him to wander about hungry.

Angus tried to persuade himself that it didn't matter too much. Perhaps just an isolated occurrence. He mustn't get obsessive about it. After all, she'd kept off the bottle for years, hadn't she?

During the next few months there was no repetition of the incident and Angus decided to forget his fear. But then it happened again. And yet again. By the time Louis was five it was a regular occurrence, and Angus didn't know what to do. Should he insist that Louis be sent to Kintalloch straight away?

Knowing how fond Nancy was of the child, Angus was afraid this would lead to a rapid deterioration in her state. Besides, he too loved the child, and wasn't looking forward to having to part with him. And how would Louis adjust to the change?

The more Angus thought about it, the more he felt Louis's

existence was due to an irresponsible whim. And then he would remember the sense of family that had possessed him at Kintalloch, and he would tell himself that this was the least he could do, his contribution to the continuation of the line.

One day he found Nancy in a more advanced state of intoxication than usual. He seized the gin bottle, which had been left on the kitchen table, and poured its content down the sink. Nancy thought this was deliciously funny. She laughed immoderately, and called Louis to come and see what Daddy was doing.

'Why is he doing that, Mummy?'

Angus found it irritating that the child was inclined to speak to his mother rather than to him, even about things that were more directly related to Angus, as on this occasion.

'Tell him. Go on, tell him,' he snapped.

Nancy swayed unsteadily to a chair and flopped down into it. 'I'll tell you, my darling, I'll tell you why Daddy'sh doing it. It'sh because he'sh nothing but a shpoilshport.' She burst into a strident laugh.

Louis, delighted, repeated:

'Shpoilshport, Daddy's a shpoilshport.' And he started marching about the room, repeating the offending words.

Angus found it unbearable to hear the child repeating the drunken pronunciation of his mother. Like a horrible foretaste of what might be to come, if Louis were left too long in Nancy's company.

Once again he considered sending Louis to Kintalloch right away. But then things settled down and again he put off the decision.

'Where's Louis?' asked Angus when he came in one afternoon.

'Sleeping.'

'Sleeping at five o'clock? Is he ill?'

'No. Just tired. I put him down on our bed.'

Angus turned towards the bedroom. It was evident that Nancy had been drinking. She had got past the euphoric stage and had now sunk into one of her ferocious glooms. This meant the child had probably had no attention for some time.

Seeing him heading for the bedroom Nancy said:

'Leave him alone. He's just tired, I tell you.' There was an edge of impatience, almost of alarm in her voice.

Angus ignored her and went into the bedroom. Louis was lying on the bed, sleeping. Angus bent over him to see him better in the dim light, then straightened up sharply. The child's breath smelt strongly of gin.

Nancy gave him a sulky look as soon as he reappeared. It was clear that she knew what to expect.

'You've been giving him gin!'

'So what? He likes it.'

'That's not what matters.'

'It matters a lot more than you think, you bloody Calvinist.'

Angus was so angry that he stood over her and said:

'If you do it again I'll kill you.'

'And what's more,' Nancy went on defiantly, 'it's never done him any harm.'

'You mean you've given him drink before?'

'So what?' This was her favourite phrase in any kind of argument. It involved no intellectual effort and invariably had the gratifying result of infuriating the opposition.

On this occasion it had its customary success. Angus raged for some time, then decided to change his tactics.

'That settles it,' he said, 'I'll make arrangements to take him over to Scotland as soon as possible.'

Instead of producing the expected argument, this statement reduced Nancy to tears. When he pointed out that she had shown herself totally unfit to look after the child she looked injured.

'All I did was give him what he wanted. He loves the stuff. All right, perhaps I gave him a little too much this time. But he'll be all right, he'll sleep it off.'

Angus was adamant. He realized later that he shouldn't have argued with her. If he'd only appeared to let things ride and then gone ahead and made the arrangements, all would have been well. He could have slipped off with the child when the time came and Nancy would have known nothing about it till it was too late.

Instead, he let habit prevail, and they argued and insulted each other, going over all the old grievances again and again. Finally he decided to put an end to the argument.

'I'm not going to discuss it any more,' he said, 'I'm sending the child to Kintalloch, and there's nothing you can do to stop me.'

Nancy gave him a look of the deepest scorn, got up and walked out of the room. A moment later he heard her closing the bedroom door behind her and turning the key in the lock. He found this a little disturbing. Why should she want to lock herself into the bedroom beside the sleeping child? Then he heard an odd sound he couldn't identify at first. Suddenly it struck him that it was the sound of furniture being moved. He got up and walked over to the bedroom door. He was greeted by a laugh from Nancy.

'You'll see if there's nothing I can do about it,' she called out. 'Try and get him now.'

What's she up to now? he wondered. Does she think all she has to do is barricade herself in with the child? She can't stay there for ever.

Still, it was a bit disquieting. If he didn't manage to talk her into opening up, sooner or later the door would have to be forced. The child couldn't be left there indefinitely with a mother whose behaviour was proving increasingly deranged.

He stood outside the bedroom door, trying to reason with her. All he got in reply was an occasional, almost hysterical laugh.

After a long silence she spoke.

'If you want to speak to me,' she said, 'you can go out on the living-room balcony. I'll speak to you from this one, and tell you what I've decided.'

Decided! thought Angus. She's hardly in a position to decide anything. And certainly not in a fit state to make any decisions. He went back into the living room and opened the glass door that led to the balcony.

In a moment Nancy appeared on the other one. She had picked up the sleeping child and slung him over one of her shoulders. His head and arms dangled down her back, while she held his legs firmly against her. He was sleeping so soundly that he seemed unaware of being moved.

'For God's sake, put that child down!'

'Why should I? He's all right.'

'He can't be, not held like that when he's sleeping. Besides, it's dangerous up here. Suppose he struggled suddenly and you dropped him?'

'Dropped him?' she said, and she laughed. 'Dropped him, that's good. Just suppose I dropped him, what then?'

'Nancy, for God's sake, have you gone mad?'

She ignored this and said:

'Have you forgotten what we're out here for? I've to tell you what I've decided. Or are you not interested? Can I do what I like with him?'

Trying to control his anger and his mounting apprehension Angus told her to go ahead:

'Tell me what you've decided.'

'That's better,' she said. 'You're so good at expecting other people to be reasonable, it's nice to see you that way for a change.'

'Well? What's your decision?'

'Oh, yes. My decision. Of course. Do you know, I'd almost forgotten? After all, it doesn't much matter to me whether I tell you or not. And then, there's no hurry, is there? We can stay here all evening – all night, if we want to. If I want to, that is. No hurry at all.'

She started swaying gently to and fro, humming snatches of song.

'Nancy, for Christ's sake, will you come to your senses?'

194

'I have,' she said. 'I've come to my senses all right. I've realized at last how to get the whip hand. So you must forgive me if I play a bit of cat and mouse with you. It makes such a change, having me at the steering wheel. And you've just got to stand there and take it, because you know that if you annoy me, all I have to do is lean forward a little, like this, and then let go . . . and then we have no more arguments about what's to happen to Louis. It will have happened, once and for all.'

Angus was eyeing the distance between the two balconies. They were about two yards apart. He thought he might just be able to jump it. But there was a drop of five storeys between them and the ground. If he missed he would have done nothing to protect the child. And anyway, by the time he had climbed on to the parapet, jumped and tried to seize the child, Nancy would have had plenty of time to carry out her threat.

He tried to consider his options, and discovered he had none. Even if he could batter his way into the bedroom and rush the balcony, Nancy might well have dropped the child into the street by then, if that was really what she meant to do. For the same reason, Angus couldn't even call out to the neighbours, as that alone might goad her into drastic action. All he could do was hope against hope that she didn't really mean what she was saying, that this was just another example of her bravado technique, and that in the end she'd get tired of the game and take the child indoors.

Much as he yearned to believe this, Angus felt he daren't. Nancy's behaviour today was so utterly out of character that he was afraid she was sufficiently insane to carry out her threat. Up till now, in her bad moods, she had been lachrymose, vituperative, passively obstructive. But to take action as she had done, barricading herself and the child into the bedroom, was something so totally unexpected that he simply could not assume it would go no further.

He decided he must approach the situation as if it were a siege. If he stood there long enough, talking, and this seemed to be what Nancy wanted, he might tire her out. Then perhaps she might take Louis back into the bedroom. He could then put a plank between the two balconies and cross over. Once he was in the bedroom he was sure he could overpower Nancy easily.

Meanwhile, he wasn't in the bedroom, and his only hope was to keep Nancy talking. He was prepared to say anything, discuss anything, promise anything, feeling that the danger to the child was such as to exonerate him in the case of any broken promises. For he felt sure that, whatever happened now, he could not possibly leave Nancy in charge of Louis ever again. His mistake, he realized now, had been in letting her see that he meant to send the boy away without further delay.

'Right, Nancy, you've got the whip hand,' he said. 'Tell me what it is you want.'

'That's asking a lot. And I want a lot. And I've never had very much, have I? I know you'll say I've got a lot more now than I had before. True enough, I suppose. But think of the price I've paid.'

'What price?'

'First, having to have a child I didn't want. Then the threat of having the child taken from me, now that I want it. And all the time your bloody preaching to put up with.'

'Right then, I'll stop preaching. I promise. Will that help?'

'A little. But not enough.'

'What else do you want? A promise that Louis can stay here?'

'I want more than a promise. Why should I believe anything you promise at this moment – now, when, as you agree, I've got the whip hand? What I need is a guarantee.'

'Well then, what guarantee can I give?'

'You can't, that's the problem. All you can do is make a promise. And how do I know you'll stick to it?'

'Then what do you want?'

'Oh, God, I don't know. I just want everything to be different. You, me . . . everything.'

'Even Louis?'

'No, he's all right. He's the only one that is. The only one of us that's worth anything.'

'Then you can't possibly mean to do him any harm.'

'No, of course not.'

'But you've just threatened to drop him over the balcony.'

'That won't do him any harm. It'll just kill him. Nothing wrong with that.'

'Most people would say there was a lot wrong with it. Nobody wants to die. I'm sure Louis doesn't.'

'He won't know. He won't even wake up. Isn't that the best thing that can happen to anybody, just to fall asleep and not wake up?'

In spite of his fear and sense of nightmare, Angus felt a wave of pity for Nancy sweep over him.

'Oh, Nancy, Nancy,' he said, 'let's try again. Let's try to get it right this time, for you as well as for Louis. Let's try again.'

Deranged as she was, Nancy felt the tenderness in his voice.

'It's too late,' she said softly, 'too late now.'

He was about to protest that it was never too late when she spoke again:

'I'm getting very tired,' she said. 'Tired of standing here holding the child, and just tired of it all. Of everything. I'll tell you what I've decided. I've decided to give you a sporting chance. In a minute I'm going to throw Louis over to you. If you can catch him, he's yours. If you can't, he's mine.'

'If I can't catch him he's dead, not yours. Can't you see that?'

'Same thing. Because after I throw him, whether you catch him or not, I'm going to jump. And no-one's going to get the chance of catching me.'

Angus was now certain she meant to carry out her threat. He looked about him to see whether there was anything on the balcony, heavy enough and near enough to let him brace his legs against, so that he could lean out as far as possible, if

197

Nancy really did throw the child. He noticed a large mosaic pot that had had plants in it long ago. They kept forgetting to water them, and the plants had all died. But the pot was full of soil, so quite heavy. It might do.

Suddenly Nancy called out:

'Here, catch!' and leaned forward over the balustrade with the intention of throwing the child. But her sudden movement wakened Louis. With a cry of terror he grabbed his mother's dress and a handful of her hair.

'Ouch, you little brute,' she cried, trying to shake him off.

Seeing his chance, Angus swiftly stepped from the mosaic pot to the balustrade and leapt across to the other balcony. He landed on top of the struggling pair, and all three rolled on the floor. Seizing the screaming child he stood up, hugging it close to him. Only then did he glance again at Nancy.

While he was occupied with the child she had managed to straddle the parapet. Angus was just in time to see her second leg swing over it. Louis was screaming so loudly that Angus didn't hear the impact of Nancy's body on the pavement. Pressing the child's face to his shoulder to keep him from seeing, Angus looked over. Five floors down, Nancy's corpse was lying spread-eagled on the pavement. People were already running towards her from different directions.

Still carrying Louis, Angus rushed out of the flat.

The child's screaming had disturbed the neighbours, and doors were opening on all the landings. Thrusting the child into the arms of one of the women, Angus ran down the stairs.

By the time he reached the street quite a little crowd had formed, and an *agent* was on the scene.

31

The telegram from Paris threw the Kintalloch household into
a flurry of surprise, apprehension, expectation and conjecture.
Angus had said nothing about sending Louis in the near future,
so it was clear that something unexpected had happened. Try as
they would, they could find no explanation that didn't involve
some catastrophe. They consoled themselves with the thought
that the child must be all right, or the journey would be out
of the question; and as Angus himself had sent the telegram,
presumably there was nothing seriously wrong with him.

That left Nancy.

Perhaps she was ill, or had had an accident? Nobody put
it into words, but they were all relieved to think that, if a
misfortune had occurred, it was almost certain that the victim
was Nancy.

Meg's immediate reaction was that she and Gavin should go.
The others refused to contemplate this, as Meg had twisted her
ankle quite badly the previous day when out walking, and they
insisted that she couldn't possibly tackle the journey.

'I'll manage all right on my own,' said Gavin.

'But the child, Gavin, think of the child. He must have
someone to take the place of his mother. I simply *must* go.'
Meg wasn't going to give in readily.

Bessie joined in. 'I think Meg's right. The child needs a
woman there, on the journey. He's bound to miss his mother.'

Meg looked at her mother-in-law gratefully, but her gratitude
turned to reproach at Bessie's next words.

'I'll go with you, Gavin. Meg and Tom can stay here and look
after each other.'

The two men agreed, and Meg had to give in.

Up till now she had accepted her injury philosophically. It
meant a few days hobbling about the house in some pain, but

nothing more. And thinking of that splendid walk made the twisted ankle seem almost worthwhile.

For some time after her mother's death Meg had given up the habit of long walks. Then she had started again, but the walking had quite a different character. Ellen had usually walked in silence, looking straight ahead, and not stopping for anything. When she started going out again, Meg's mind was on the future arrival of Louis, and she started paying more attention to everything round about her, to be equipped to show the child all the things that only a knowledgeable eye can see. So she examined the hedgerows, looking for nests, watching the birds and small animals that up till then she, as a town-bred girl, had never really observed. She was rewarded by discovering a completely new and fascinating world. She would come home full of queries, sometimes bringing a little trophy – a stone, a twig, a piece of eggshell – for identification.

The others teased her about this. 'Meg's just discovered Nature,' they would say.

On the present day, unexpectedly mild, she had followed the path up the glen, right to the col. From there she was able to look down into the next valley, a world she had never before seen from above. She was coming back, hurrying a little, for she had gone further than she had originally meant and it was getting late. She was walking joyfully among heaped up autumn leaves, when she stood on a stone hidden by the leaves. Her foot slipped and was caught between that stone and another, equally big. She was walking too fast to be able to stop herself right away, and she fell, jerking her ankle badly.

It was so painful that at first she thought she wouldn't be able to walk at all. Luckily she had told Bessie where she was going. Tom always insisted that she must not go out on her own without making sure someone in the household knew what direction she was taking. So far she had found this an annoying constraint, but had submitted to it. Now she began to realize that she might be very thankful indeed that someone knew where to look for her. After resting for a while she found she was able to limp along, very slowly. It seemed an interminably long way back to the house, and she wished she had taken Tom's advice and brought a stick. She still had some distance to go when she saw Gavin approaching. Bessie had noticed Meg's prolonged absence, and had sent him off to look for her.

Her gratitude for the support system that the family provided was still lively the following day, and kept her from arguing too much about going with Gavin to collect Louis. After all, she really had been near the point of collapse when Gavin turned up.

Barely an hour after the arrival of the telegram the travellers were on their way. Tom and Meg were left sitting by the fire, debating what could possibly have happened in Paris. Half-way through the evening Meg looked up with a little laugh and said:

'I've just thought of something.' Then she started to get up.

'Sit still,' commanded Tom. 'I can get whatever it is. What do you want?'

'My coat.'

'Your coat? You're not cold, are you? Let's get some more coal on the fire.'

'No, no, I'm not cold. There's something in my coat pocket I'd forgotten about. It might come in handy. You'll find the coat in the back cloakroom. But don't bother to bring it. Just put your hand in the right-hand pocket and bring what you'll find there.'

Tom came back in a moment holding a little branch with three tiny, perfect fir cones on it.

'Lovely, isn't it?' said Meg.

'Yes. For Louis, I suppose?'

'That's right. Only I didn't know it when I picked the thing up.'

'That reminds me,' said Tom, and left the room. He came back in a few minutes carrying a large rocking-horse.

'I remember that!' exclaimed Meg. 'We used to play on it when I came here for the holidays. He'll love that, surely. Where has it been all these years?'

'In hiding, in a cupboard in my dressing room. I always rather liked it, and decided to rescue it from one of Bessie's clearing-out sessions. She must have know it was there – nothing escapes her eagle eye. But she's evidently respected my unspoken wishes in the matter, and there it has stayed all these years. But we'll need more toys, won't we?'

'Yes, of course we will. This has been a childless house too long.'

'Tell you what,' said Tom, 'you and I can have a little expedition tomorrow. A run in the car won't do your ankle any harm, will it?'

'And I've thought of something else,' added Meg. 'We'll need to get a room ready for Louis, won't we?'

'That's your province. You're sole mistress of Kintalloch for the time being.'

The words brought a little thrill to Meg. Even if only for a day or two, she was in charge. And with Louis here things were going to be totally different. She remembered the feeling she had had nearly all her life, of waiting for *real* life to start. It looked as if the time had come at last.

Bessie and Gavin brought back an extremely frightened, shocked and hostile child. Although he had been brought up to speak English and French with equal ease, he had refused to speak anything but French since his mother's death. Gavin and Bessie had found this quite a strain. They saw it as a rejection of themselves and all they stood for. But they did their best, with the limited French available to them, and tried to make a joke of it.

'Mum's vocabulary has increased enormously during the trip,' said Gavin.

'Yes, I can now say *dodo, pipi* and *dada.*'

'That's right,' agreed her son. 'She can manage words of two syllables, provided they're the same one repeated. Advanced stuff!'

Louis was hiding his face in Bessie's skirt. He had accepted her, but would have nothing to do with Gavin. Perhaps he found him too like Angus. Since the scuffle on the balcony he had shown an extreme aversion to his father, as if he thought him responsible for what had happened.

This was what had prompted Angus to send for the others right away. He hoped that in time Louis would forget that terrible evening and accept his presence without the aversion that it evidently inspired. But as long as he was in the flat there seemed to be no possibility of his forgetting his mother. He spent all the time going from one room to the other, asking for *Maman*.

They were all standing in the hall, not knowing what to do to make the child feel at home. Meg and Tom still didn't know what had happened. As long as they were in the child's presence no such communication was possible, for he understood English perfectly, though still refusing to speak it. At this moment he wasn't even responding to appeals in French. Meg had tried speaking to him, as had the others, but with equally little success. Then she thought of the rocking horse.

'Viens, mon chéri, j'ai un dada pour toi.'

The little boy looked up, saw Meg's outstretched hand, and took it. She led him to the room they had prepared for him. The ancient horse stood in the middle of the room, its head as tall as Louis's. The child walked guardedly towards it, then looked enquiringly at Meg. She smiled.

'C'est pour toi, mon petit.'

Shyly the little boy went right up to the horse, put his arms round its neck, and sank his face into its mane. Meg stood by in silence.

It was months before the boy got over his fear and suspicion and settled down happily in his new home. Bessie and Meg he accepted fairly quickly, but he took a long time to show anything but distrust of the two men. In the end he accepted them too, and Gavin started taking him round the property every morning, just as his father and his grandfather had done with their sons. Once a year Angus came and tried to establish a good relationship with the boy. But Louis was always distant with him, and soon escaped from his presence.

When Louis was ten Angus came for the last time. On this occasion his son challenged him.

'Why do you keep coming here?' he asked. 'Nobody wants you here. Nobody needs you.'

'I come to see you. Remember I'm your father, and I love you and miss you.'

'Well, I don't love you or miss you. And what's more,' the child added with sudden passion, 'you're *not* my father. Uncle Gavin's my father. I know that sounds silly, but you know what I mean.'

'You would rather I didn't come back?'

Louis looked at him sullenly, but made no reply. Angus was left in no doubt as to his meaning.

He said nothing to the others about this conversation, and felt certain the boy wouldn't say anything either, ashamed of his frankness.

Not long afterwards Angus wrote to Bessie that he was off to Spain, to fight in the International Brigade. That was the last she ever heard of him.

32

The men were scattered about the floor of the room, kneeling, squatting, sitting cross-legged, peering at their cards in the dim light of the single paraffin lamp. One of them looked up when Angus appeared in the doorway.

'Want a game?'

'No thanks.' Then, afraid of sounding too churlish, he added: 'Too tired, even for cards.' He crossed the room and sat down on the wooden bench near the fireplace, holding out his hands to the meagre warmth.

'You'd think he was the only one who'd tramped twenty miles today,' muttered one of the players.

'Well, he's just too old for this sort of thing. Must be forty if he's a day.'

Angus caught some of the words, and guessed the rest. Boys, he thought in disgust, mere boys. What do they know? Come out here with their adolescent ideals, flying the Communist flag, ready to save Spain from the Fascists. Not a man among them, except for Bob, and he's just as bad as they are. Can't open his mouth without quoting Marx at you. And anyway, I'm not forty yet. They didn't even get that right.

A figure detached itself from one of the groups and came over to stand in front of the fire beside Angus. For a moment the two men looked at each other in silence. It was Bob who spoke first:

'I sometimes wonder what the hell you're doing here,' he said.

'Same as the rest of you, I suppose.'

'I doubt it. We're here to fight for a cause.'

'And I'm not?'

'Well, are you?'

Angus gave an exasperated sigh. 'What does it matter what I'm here for, anyway? I do what we're all expected to do, don't

I? I fight when I get the chance, I tramp miles and miles when we have to retreat – and when do we do anything else? I'm half frozen and half starved, like the rest of you. What more do you want?'

'That's not how to win a war.'

'You don't have to tell me that. I'm not giving the orders, am I?'

'That isn't what I meant. It's your attitude that's wrong.'

'Well, it's *my* attitude, isn't it? It's not doing anyone any harm.'

'Yes, it is. There's no room for Romantic gestures here.'

'You sound as if I was pretending to be Lord Byron.'

'Far from it. He was at least fighting for an ideal. God alone knows what you're looking for here.'

'I'll tell you. I'm looking for a bullet.'

'That's just what I thought. There's your Romantic gesture for you. And that's why you've no right to be here.'

'No *right!* What the hell do you mean? I've as much bloody right as the rest of you.'

'No, you haven't. You don't give a damn about the people of Spain. You don't give a damn about progress or politics or anything, not even the very men you're fighting beside. You're just here for your own purposes. You're no better than a bloody mercenary.'

Angus stood up, ready to hit Bob, then thought better of it. 'What's the point?' he muttered scornfully, brushed past the other man and left the room. He made his way up to the loft in darkness and lay down on the straw, pulling some of it over him to act as a bedcover.

He lay still for a long time, telling himself that with the warmth of the straw covering he would soon be asleep. It was certainly an improvement on the accommodation they had had for some time. But he was too angry to sleep – too angry and too deeply discouraged. He thought over what Bob had said and began to feel his anger draining away.

For it was Bob, after all, who had got it right. Angus had to admit to himself that he certainly hadn't come here to defend the Spanish Republic. He had come because he felt miserable and rejected and utterly aimless. And that bit about looking for a bullet! He now felt ashamed of its melodramatic overtones. And it wasn't even true, come to think of it. If it was really death he wanted he could have found a quicker and more certain way. He could, after all, have provided his own bullet; or jumped from a fifth floor balcony, like Nancy. But that, of course, would have been an admission of total defeat.

And that wasn't really what he wanted.

One thing he did want was to make the Kintalloch family squirm. Make them realize what a wonderful, self-sacrificing character he was, giving his life in a noble cause. The supreme Romantic gesture, in fact.

Bob had been right.

It was the second winter of the Civil War, and the first since Angus had joined the International Brigade. He hadn't known what to expect, and had thought he was just about ready for anything. As it turned out, the one big surprise had been the cold. Up till his arrival in Spain his ideas about the country had been strictly Mediterranean. He had expected sunshine and palm trees, and hot, still nights. Instead he had found the cold and the snow and the bitter winds of the high mountains of Aragon.

The campaign so far had been mainly a matter of long spells of waiting, interrupted by tactical retreats. But they had seen some action, and in a recent skirmish he and his companions had been cut off from the rest of their company. They were now trying to meet up with them again, with no knowledge of the austere country they were in, and only a vague idea of where to head for. Last night had been spent in the open, sheltering in a deep gully. Tonight things were better. They had taken over an abandoned farmhouse. Tomorrow they would set off again, looking for either the enemy or their own company. It didn't seem to matter very much which. Either would at least deliver them from this limbo in which they now wandered through mountains every bit as hostile as the enemy.

Angus had such a restless night that he was glad to get up at dawn and make his way down to the big room on the ground floor. The place looked forlorn and deserted in the cold grey light. He wandered over to a window to inspect the surrounding scenery and was surprised to see nothing but white. The snow was falling so thickly that he could only dimly make out the threatening form of the mountain in front. He stood at the window for a long time, hypnotised by this white dancing world outside. After a while he was aware of nothing but the falling snow, feeling nothing, thinking nothing, remembering nothing. When at last he was called back to the present by the sound of steps on the stairs he felt refreshed and renewed, almost as if he had slept all night. He knew what he had to do, and hoped Bob would come down soon.

It was in fact Bob who now appeared. Angus greeted him with the words:

'You were right last night. I see I've been attitudinising.'

Just then some of the men came clattering down the stairs. All Bob could say, as the others burst out in excitement at the sight of the blizzard, was:

'We'll talk later.'

'Come on, boys, bring your skis!' whooped one of the younger men.

'Anyone for snowballs?'

'Christmas is coming, the goose is getting fat,' sang out another ironically.

Bob hadn't noticed the snow till the other men drew his attention to it with their merriment.

'Young idiots,' he said sternly. 'What do we do now?' He turned to Angus, who shook his head.

'Damned if I know,' was all he could offer.

There were no officers, not even an NCO among the little

group, and the men had spontaneously turned to Bob as their leader. Though a few years younger than Angus he was much older than the others, and had accepted his position without question. It had seemed natural that, of the two older men, it was Bob the youngsters had turned to in search of a leader. After all, Bob shared their ideals, whereas he, Angus, manifestly didn't. Now it occurred to him that the choice had perhaps also been made because of Bob's personal qualities. He was serious but approachable – and Angus had to admit that since joining the company he himself had displayed none of the latter quality. If Bob's virtues had played their part in the choice, it was also highly probable that Angus's limitations had also counted for something. He had been too taken up with his own grief and resentment right from the start to let them see anything but the darker side of his nature. He had done what was required of him, had taken care not to quarrel with any of them, but had made no effort to conceal the fact that he shared neither their youthful high spirits nor their ideals.

In his present mood of self-abasement he was anxious to show Bob that he was willing to cooperate.

'Shall I get the others down, so that you can discuss the problem with them?'

'Yes, I think we'd better. If we're leaving we'll have to go soon. The days are short enough anyway, even without a blizzard to reckon with.'

Angus climbed back up to the loft and roused the last few sleepers. He made it clear that he was acting on Bob's orders, feeling sure that they would pay little attention to him otherwise.

'It's like this,' said Bob once the men were all gathered together. 'These mountains are bad enough to tackle even without all this snow. As things are at present, it would be very risky to set out. We might wander about for days without finding shelter. On the other hand, there's no food here. If we knew the storm would be over tomorrow it would be worth waiting. But we've no idea how long it may last. So what do we do? Any suggestions?'

No, there were no suggestions. The seriousness of the situation had got through to even the most optimistic of the men.

'Looks like you're going to have to decide,' said Angus.

'Well, somebody's got to. So what's it to be? Do we go or do we wait here?'

There was a silence. Bob turned to Angus.

'What do you think?'

'I think waiting's the most difficult thing to do on this earth.' Angus spoke quietly, almost as if to himself. But it was enough. The men suddenly started talking, each saying what he thought. It was clear that most of them wanted to make a move. No, they didn't know where they were, they didn't know which way to go; but if you just keep on going downhill, it's bound to take you somewhere, isn't it? Somewhere with houses and people, and perhaps even food.

They set off. Bob was in the lead, having asked Angus to bring up the rear. 'Just make sure nobody drops out, will you? It's going to be tough going, so we've simply got to keep together. Right?'

'Right,' answered Angus, glad to be given a job to do, and relieved that the talk with Bob would have to wait for a while. There was a lot he wanted to discuss, but felt it would be better to wait till their new relationship had had time to consolidate. While he was ready to admit that his attitude so far had been wrong, perhaps even childish, he knew that any serious conversation with Bob would be bound to bring in the Communist ideal, which he was not prepared to accept. Better, then, to wait till they had found a little more common ground on the human level, since that seemed to be the way things were going. After that, ideological disagreements wouldn't matter so much.

Angus now realized just how cut off from the rest of mankind he had been since his arrival in Spain some months before.

* * *

From the start he had felt different from the other men, and they
had taken him at his own valuation, and left him alone. This had
fitted in very well with his then idea of himself as a solitary
outcast. All his life he had lived in phases – there had been the
Paris phase, in which he had mingled in the intellectual life of
the city; the successive love affairs phase, culminating in his
long, tormented affair with Nancy; then the fatherhood phase,
which had finally come to an end with his son's explicit rejection
of him. Now he realized intuitively that he had a deep need of
some human contact, and Bob seemed to offer this possibility.

They struggled on all day, cold, tired and hungry. By evening
they still had no idea where they were or what they might have
achieved. They had certainly lost height, but it was difficult
to say how much, for often they had found themselves faced
with a cliff edge or a dangerous ravine, and had been obliged
to climb up again to skirt the obstacle. As the last light faded
they decided to shelter under a huge rock clinging to the side
of the mountain. It would afford them protection from the wind
and the falling snow.

'Right, boys, we'll spend the night here, under this rock,'
said Bob.

'"Come in under the shadow of this red rock,"' quoted Dick,
the Oxford undergraduate.

'Blimey, chaps, there's something wrong with young Dick,'
exclaimed one of the others. 'He thinks this here rock's red.'

'He's seeing red, that's what it is,' put in another.

Bob came up to the little group. 'What is it, Dick? You don't
really see this rock as red, do you?'

'Quotation,' said Dick. 'T. S. Eliot.'

'That's it!' exclaimed Angus. 'I recognize it now. It's from
The Waste Land.'

'Very appropriate,' remarked Bob drily.

Dick gave Angus a quick, eager look, and Angus realized he had another potential friend here. He sat down beside the boy.

'Have you read a lot of Eliot?'

'Every word he's written,' was Dick's devout reply.

'That's more than I can claim. But then, I've spent most of the last twenty years in France, and I really know more about French literature.'

'That's what I mean to do after I get my degree – go to France. Paris, of course. Or rather, that's what I meant to do. Now, with this, it's all different. No point in making plans at the moment, is there?'

'What made you volunteer? A devotion to the Communist cause doesn't seem to go all that well with Oxford and T. S. Eliot.'

'I know. It was just, somehow, I felt a bit of a heel, having such a wonderful time and knowing what was going on here. And then, I just couldn't forget they had murdered Lorca.'

'The gipsy poet?'

'Well, he wasn't a gipsy himself. For him the gipsy stood for the aristocrat – the free man, the poet. And the Nationalists murdered him. In the end I felt I just couldn't stand back any longer. I had to do something about it. So here I am.'

'I don't suppose your people were any too pleased.'

Dick sighed. 'They were terribly upset. It was awful. But what do you do, I ask you? What do you do?' There was a tremor in his voice, as if he were near to tears.

'In a conflict of loyalties, you mean?'

'Yes. How d'you know which is the right thing to do?'

Angus thought for a moment. 'Well, look at it like this. Either you do what you don't want, and then at least you're not being self-indulgent, or you do what you do want, and try to forget about the conflict.' He paused once again, while he thought over his answer to the boy's passionate demand. 'Not very helpful, is it? But then, I'm trying to be realistic.'

'I suppose', said Dick thoughtfully, 'what you mean is that some problems just don't have a solution?'

'Something like that. Most of mine don't seem to, anyway.'

It wasn't till the following evening that they at last stumbled into a small village and learned that they were still in Republican territory. After a couple of days' rest they set off again to try and get back to their company, with some provisions and a vague idea of where to head for. In fact they never made it. Soon they learned that their companions had all been killed or taken prisoner in one of the Nationalist offensives.

After that they had to put up with the most discouraging part of the whole campaign. Nobody needed them, nobody wanted them. There seemed to be no action, not even guerrilla fighting, anywhere near them. They headed for the front, feeling frustrated and unnecessary.

The news from the front was increasingly depressing. After the euphoria of capturing Teruel in January nothing else seemed to have gone right, and the insurgents recaptured it the following month. Now they had advanced as far as the Mediterranean, forming a wedge that split the Republican forces in two. In an attempt to recapture lost ground an offensive was started south of the Ebro, and the men knew that reinforcements were constantly being sent to this front.

'It's a bit like sitting an exam,' Dick said one morning, while they were waiting to hear where they were to be sent next, 'except that with an exam you usually know the date beforehand. Here you don't know a thing, just that one of these days they're going to come along with a truck and tell you to get in.'

'Makes it worse, the not knowing when, doesn't it?' said Angus.

'Well, at least you don't have to swot for this one,' was Bob's comment.

The truck came for them early one morning in September. All they knew was that they were to join a Catalan regiment stationed near the Ebro. As they set off, packed like sardines in the uncovered truck, they felt the chill of the high mountain air.

'Won't be like this by the time we get down there,' said one of them. 'It's hot as hell in the Ebro valley.'

'Can't say I'll be sorry to see the last of these damn mountains,' remarked Bob.

'You don't like mountains?' Dick sounded shocked. 'And yet you live near the Lake District.'

'Oh, they're all right in moderation. But this is beyond a joke.'

'Well, I can't say there's anything very moderate about the Pyrenees. But I like them all the same,' said Angus.

'That's because you're used to your Scottish mountains.'

Angus laughed. 'They're nothing like this. You could drop Ben Nevis in among this lot and you'd never even notice it.'

Dick was gazing with awe at the panorama unfolding before them as the truck slowly climbed up the twisting road. 'I think this is utterly magnificent. Never seen anything like it. When this business is over I'd like to come back, just to wander about.'

'You'd think you'd done enough wandering about mountains last winter in the middle of a blizzard.'

'Well, that was the problem. You can't see much in the middle of a blizzard. But on a lovely clear day like this . . . '

'Clear day or not,' replied Bob, 'I'll be glad to see the last of these monsters.'

A while later he turned to Angus and handed him a slip of paper. 'That's my parents' address. Just in case. Will you go and see them?'

'Of course. If I can. Any message?'

'Just tell them . . . ' Bob stopped, then shook his head helplessly.

'I'll tell them,' said Angus.

A moment later Bob spoke again. 'If it's the other way round, would you like me to go to Kintalloch?'

Angus shook his head. 'No point,' was all he said.

They were coasting down hill into a high, shallow valley when the driver jammed on the brakes.

'Jump, boys, and scatter,' he yelled, just as they saw a couple of planes approaching. They all leapt out and made for whatever shelter they could find in the rocky, barren landscape.

Angus lay down close to a big rock, and Bob flung himself under a stunted bush a few feet away. The planes dived down over them, their machine guns firing, then roared up again into the sky. Angus crawled over to Bob, and found him lying on his back. A large red stain had appeared on his chest, and he was breathing with difficulty. Angus put his arm under his shoulder and raised him a little to try and ease the breathing.

'No use,' Bob whispered. Then he added, 'Bloody mountains . . . ' He closed his eyes, then opened them again and looked about him wildly. 'Where's Dick?' he said in a faint voice.

'I'll find him. Don't worry. I'll look after him.'

Bob smiled and nodded. Then a spasm shook his body, he coughed and a wave of blood streamed out of his mouth. His head fell back, his whole body went limp, and Angus realized that he was dead. He put him down gently and stood up. All he could think of was that he had promised to look for Dick.

'Dick!' he called. 'Dick! Are you all right?'

A voice yelled:

'Get down, you fool. They're coming back.'

Angus stood still as he watched the planes screaming towards him. 'Must find Dick,' he thought, and took a step forward. A moment later the planes were over him, firing, and he fell to the ground.

After the planes had gone the survivors crawled out of what little shelter they had found and began picking up the casualties and lifting them into the truck.

'What about the dead?' asked one of the men.

The officer in charge shook his head.

'No time,' he said, 'we'll just have to leave them. Those buggers might be back any minute.'

He looked at the inert figures of Bob and Angus, sighed, and turned back to the truck.

33

'My life has been studded with wars,' said Bessie. 'First the Boer War, when I was young. Then the Great War. That one took both my sons away, but at least let me have them back later. Now we're hardly finished with the Spanish Civil War – which took Angus for good – and here we go again. If we can't get Hitler finished off quickly, it'll be Louis's turn to go.'

'Oh, come on Mum, he's only thirteen,' protested Gavin. 'It'll all be over long before he's old enough to be called up.'

'To volunteer, you mean,' corrected Louis. 'I'm not going to sit around waiting to be called up.'

Bessie sighed. 'God knows how long it may last.'

Meg looked at her mother-in-law with some concern. It wasn't like Bessie to be so gloomy. Certainly Angus's disappearance in Spain had shaken both her and Tom, but all the same she had never known Bessie complain or take a pessimistic attitude. In all the trials and tribulations the family had gone through Bessie could be counted on to remain cheerful and efficient. I suppose she's getting old, Meg thought. Still, Uncle Tom's a year or two older, and he hasn't changed in the last twenty years. But then, he's led a very retired life all that time. Perhaps Aunt Bessie has worn herself out. She's been so active all her life.

For the first time Meg faced the possibility that soon they might have to get on without Bessie. It seemed to her that Bessie was the heart of the household. She remembered her own early married life, and the feeling of being kept in the background while Bessie made all the decisions, and she smiled at the thought of how inadequately she would have acquitted herself if she had had to run the house.

Now, of course, it was different. She felt she had become a

reasonably competent housekeeper. Thanks to Aunt Bessie, of course, she thought, and reflected on how little she had learnt in that respect from her mother.

And then she smiled, thinking of the contrast between these two women who had shaped her life. Although Ellen had never uttered any criticism of Bessie, Meg had always felt she didn't appreciate her sister-in-law as others did. After reading the poems and finding out about her mother's passionate attachment to Tom she thought she might have found the reason. But perhaps it was just a case of her mother's aristocratic reserve being ruffled by Aunt Bessie's almost animal *joie de vivre*. Much as she had loved her mother, she couldn't help reflecting that Bessie would be missed far more, if indeed she was nearing the end of her life. Perhaps there had been too many blows for her lately, what with Angus's disappearance, Doc's death the following year, and now another war.

As time went by Bessie showed no signs of recovering her spirits or her energy. The family did what they could to cheer her up, and never admitted to each other that the old, indomitable Bessie had gone. She struggled on till the second winter of the war. Then she fell victim to an influenza epidemic, and died within a few days.

Tom took the loss of his wife with surprising stoicism. He spoke of her frequently, recalling her good qualities and the good times they had had together. He mourned, but with serenity, and sometimes said it was just a question of filling in the time for a year or two, and then they would be together again. He was not a religious-minded man – none of the Lindsay family were – but he seemed to take it as absolutely certain that he and Bessie would be reunited, and this sustained him. At first Meg and Gavin had feared the blow would be too much for his already fragile health. However, the weak reed bowed under the storm, but did not break.

On one occasion Tom and Meg were sitting by the fire, and

he was talking about Bessie and all he owed to her. Pensively, more as if talking to himself than to Meg, he said:

'God knows what might have become of me if she hadn't taken it into her head to marry me. That was my salvation.'

'From what?' asked Meg, not sure whether to speak.

'From myself, I suppose. From a great danger I was in. Bessie saved me.' Then he gave a little laugh, as if to shake off the meditative mood. 'And all because she wanted to be mistress of Kintalloch!'

Was he thinking of her mother? Had he felt in danger of yielding to her incestuous desire? That was the nearest Meg ever came to learning the truth of the matter.

Bessie's foreboding proved right, and the war dragged on long enough to engulf Louis in its last year. Luckily he was not posted abroad, and was able to come home on leave at intervals.

One day in 1946 Meg spent the afternoon moving restlessly about the house, from the upstairs hall down to the sitting room where Tom was waiting, then back upstairs again, looking eagerly for the first sign of the car that was to bring Louis home for good. Gavin had gone to meet him in Edinburgh, and Meg had decided to stay in order to keep Tom company. In a way she preferred to greet Louis here, in the house. It reminded her of the two previous occasions when she had stayed at home waiting for news of him, first when they were waiting for the telegram that was to announce his birth, and next, five years later, when Bessie and Gavin had brought him home from Paris.

Yes, home, she thought. It *is* his home and he loves it and always has, after the first few terrible weeks when he was still grieving over the loss of his mother. Now, she felt absolutely sure, he accepted her and Gavin as his parents.

At any rate, she knew that he had filled the place of a son in her life. Since Louis's arrival the sense of emptiness had gone. Even when he was away, first at school and then in the army, she had missed him, she had worried over him, but she had never felt that deadening emptiness in herself. Thinking of what Louis meant to them all, she realized that he was a link between Tom and Ellen. Knowing what she did about her mother's feelings for Tom, she could now understand why Ellen had looked forward so eagerly to having a grandson, an innocent and living embodiment of her love. Louis, if not actually her grandson, could be considered her grandson by adoption. What a pity she never knew him, thought Meg. What a pity she can't see my fulfilment as a mother. But if ghosts exist, I'm sure hers must haunt Kintalloch, and be comforted by the presence of her beloved brother's grandson.

'The train must be late,' said Tom, 'they should have been here by now.'

'Yes, I know. But they're often late these days. We're not back to pre-war conditions yet, you know.'

Meg went back upstairs, looking out for the black car on the bare stretch of road before the turn into the drive. She let her eyes rest on the late afternoon light as it lay on the hills. The deeper parts of the glen were already in shadow, but she knew the sun would rest on the upper slopes of the hills for a long time yet. It had taken her years, many years, she reflected, to learn to look at the hills properly. All her early life she had been so engrossed with her inner landscape that she had really seen nothing of what was about her, and this had added to her emptiness.

She thought of the feeling of waiting for life to begin that had haunted her during her early years. Her premonition had been right, the arrival of Louis had put an end to that, filling her with a sense of purpose, a feeling of being needed, which nothing, not even her marriage, had given her before. And yet, it had been a happy marriage, once she had got over her misery over the loss of her babies, and the terrible months when she had thought her life could only be bearable beside Angus. How right he had been to go away!

For the first time she realized that her happiness and fulfilment in having Louis as her long-awaited child were due entirely to the way this episode in her life had concluded. If Angus hadn't gone back to Paris there would have been no Louis; and it was because of his remorse over the way he had left her that he had arranged for the child to come to Kintalloch. How odd, she thought, how odd that I've never realized this before. And if Angus hadn't gone back and later sent them the promise of the child, her own marriage would never have settled into the calm, companionable relationship that had for many years now united her and Gavin. She might just have gone on seeing Gavin as the man she was bound to, but nothing more. She would never have known what an excellent surrogate father he made.

This consideration led her to wonder whether, all those years ago, when she had lost one child after another, she had failed to appreciate the sorrow this must have caused Gavin; and she felt thankful that he too had benefited so greatly from the presence of their nephew. She had realized, of course, that the loss of an heir to Kintalloch must have been tragic for Gavin; but it had not struck her at the time that he must also have been grieving over the personal loss this entailed.

One of her happiest memories was of the day that Louis finally made it clear that Gavin was accepted. From the beginning Gavin had suggested that the child should come with him in the morning when he set out on his rounds of the estate, and Louis had refused. Every morning Gavin said:

'Coming, Louis?'

And Louis shook his head and stayed behind with the women. But after a few months he started following Gavin, keeping a few cautious steps behind him, but showing an interest in what was going on. Gradually the distance between the man and the little boy shortened, till one day, when Gavin issued his usual invitation, Louis had run up to him and taken his hand. As they walked off together Gavin had turned to look at Meg. She had never forgotten the expression of joy and pride on her husband's face at that moment.

In her mellow mood it seemed to her that everything in her life had worked together for the happy outcome of all her troubles. Her guilty love for Angus had been transformed into her innocent and fruitful caring for his orphaned son. And if Angus could see the handsome and charming young man that this son had turned into, he would be proud of him. Even the rancour that Louis had felt towards Angus seemed to have faded and been replaced by a sort of hero-worship for the father who had died fighting for a cause.

Poor Angus, she thought, lying dead and probably unburied on a Spanish mountain side. He had always been so full of life, so intense, so passionately alive, that she still found it hard to think of him as dead.

As her thoughts returned to the present, she looked at the level light on the hills, and thought of what this familiar landscape had come to mean to her. It was largely because of Louis that she had learned to look at the world that surrounded her, during the years that she had been in training, as it were, to be a mother to this unknown child. And after he had arrived, together they had looked and examined and enquired and learned about all the wonders round about them.

'Perhaps they've had a puncture,' said Tom next time she went down to see him.

'Oh, well. If they have, they'll certainly be able to cope with it.'

Tom smiled. 'You know Meg, there are times when you remind me of Bessie.'

Meg got up and kissed him.

'I take that as a great compliment,' she said.

Restlessly she wandered upstairs again; she wasn't worried, only impatient. And she was afraid Tom was beginning to worry. Just then, as she looked out of the window she saw a black car on the stretch of road just before the turn into the drive. It slowed down to take the curve, and as it did so she saw a hand waving from the passenger's side.

'They're here, they're here,' she shouted, and ran towards the stairs.

Tom was standing in the doorway of the sitting room and called out to her as she rushed down the stairs.

'Take it easy,' he said. 'You don't want to greet them with a broken ankle, do you?'

Meg stopped on the wide Kintalloch landing and put a hand on her heart as if to quiet its pounding. As if to hold in its happiness, she thought. She was standing exactly where her mother had stood nearly seventy years before, on her seventh birthday.